without
cease
the earth
faintly

trembles

without cease

the earth faintly trembles

Amanda Marchand

First edition

New Writers Series edited by Robert Allen

Design by **conundrum**

Cover: "June" courtesy of Katie Lewandowski

Printed in Canada

National Library of Canada Cataloguing in Publication

Marchand, Amanda, 1968-
Without cease the earth faintly trembles / Amanda Marchand.

ISBN 0-919688-73-X (bound).—ISBN 0-919688-71-3 (pbk.)

I. Title.

PS8576.A63275W48 2003 C813'.6 C2003-903648-0

DC Books gratefully acknowledges the suport of The Canada Council for the Arts and of SODEC for our publishing program.

DC BOOKS / LIVRES DC
Box 662, 950 Decarie, Montreal, Quebec, H4L 4V9 Canada

I would like to acknowledge (the memory of) Kathy Acker who was there when I wrote the first of these ten years ago at the San Francisco Art Institute.

Thank you Rob Allen, Anne Stone, Francesca Lodico, John Geraci, Samar Fawaz for your support and careful reading of the manuscript. I am also grateful to Mr. Andy Brown for designing this book, as well as publishing my writing before anyone else.

Acknowledgement is made to the publishers of the following magazines, anthologies, chapbooks in which some of these pieces (often in earlier versions) previously appeared: *You and Your Bright Ideas: New Montreal Writing* (Véhicule Press), *this tastiness cannot be carried even by both hands* (Glass Eye Press), *Matrix #51*, *The Moosehead Review #6* (DC Books), *June Makes a Friend* (conundrum press), *Throat*, and *index Vol.2 #6.*

The poem *in the future* borrows from Elaine Scarry's, *On Beauty and Being Just* (Princeton, 1999). *Under the Influence* borrows from Anne Stone's chapbook, *Sweet Dick All.* "Maidenhead Revisited" (*Harper's,* May 2003) appears as a doctored fragment in *The Reverse Side of the Letter A*. The graph is according to Charles Féré (*Sensation et Mouvement*, 1887). Many other writings in this book make reference to visual art and literature. This is only a small sampling of those whose spark or voice resonates herein: Betty Goodwin, Clarice Lispector, anna gaskell, Helene Cixous, Gertrude Stein, Jean Genet, Elizabeth Smart, Mary Scott, Virginia Woolf.

Affectionate thanks go to the following people (places and things) who have, at various stages of the writing, been there: Jane Burpee, Pang Lim, the Headlands Center for the Arts, Claire Kusy, Gail Scott, Solidoro, the Montreal writing scene, Laura Baldwin, Bill Berkson, Tory Cowling (your turn), Leslie Scalapino, everyone who gave input on the cover, those from whom I've pillaged words or experiences, *Sea Echo*, Mary Janacek, and my family (including the memory of my grandmother, Maureen, who secretly and in front of large crowds, knew how to dance).

For their ultimate support and love, I would like to thank my father, and my mother who said, "I didn't know you had written a book!"

I would also like to thank Katie Lou for giving me an image to go with the words.

Witnout Cease the Eartn Faintly Trembles. 1988
Techniques mixtes, acier sur papier. 233 x 140 cm.

— Betty Goodwin, *4 collection de l'ange*

for

Jessica Bé

C o n t

Part One

ents

Line:

This is an elastic term. A line may be an edge, a meeting of areas.... It may be broad or thin, sharp or blurred, firm or wavering, tight or loose, delicate or bold, energetic or weak. Whatever its function and character, line suggests movement in some direction: each of which produces a certain emotional reaction. Lines may be continuous or broken, and when they are broken one may still feel the continuity of the movement even though the actual line is invisible. It is seldom that only one kind of line is used in a design. More likely two or more interplay, with varying degrees of harmony and contrast, like themes in a musical composition.

— Helen Gardener, *Art Through the Ages*

Part
One

The Marble Necklace

June is at a martini party and everyone is drinking vodka and vermouth martinis with pimento olives. There is a man with feathered hair in the kitchen making martini pitchers and putting the pitchers in the freezer to chill. Someone brings out a flaming chocolate cake with *Happy Birthday* written across the top in pink icing. The cake is eaten, except for a chunk left untouched on the radiator. There are people dancing in twos and threes and people crawling out the window onto the balcony. Some are not, but most of the people there are librarians.

There is a man with a monocle who arrives late. June sees him out of the corner of her eye while she is refilling her drink. A girl beside him is talking about Halitosis Lucy the dog, and laughing and repeating that she must go home soon, "or Halitosis Lucy will piss on the floor." The music is loud now. The man making martinis is shaking them and pouring them quickly and making extra pitchers. Sometimes people are dancing. Mostly people are not dancing now, but sometimes they are dancing. Mostly they are climbing out the window into the night. Another martini and June feels her body relax. She becomes aware of this, her shoulders loosening and her body limbering. She becomes conscious that she is suddenly happy sitting on this long couch between other people. She says to the person beside her, "I would like to stay here forever and never leave, just have this party go on forever like this, all these — " and she looks around the room, and for a moment she is truly happy. She feels flushed. Perhaps it is the vodka but she feels warm inside this smoky place, sitting on the long sofa, almost as if this were her true family from the family of man.

Then suddenly everyone is clambering out the window onto the balcony. The couples that were sometimes dancing have climbed outside onto the balcony, and everyone is sliding up the narrow fire escape to the rooftop. The roof has no ledge to guard against falling off, and it is cool outside, and drizzling. People cluster in groups, joking and smoking. June feels the sides dragging her over, dragging at her clothes as if an underwater current, and it is not a safe feeling like the feeling on the sofa but a terrible feeling. Nothing is there to stop her from jumping off the edge. *The Edge Of The World* is there in front of her — she had always known the world wasn't truly round. Right in front of her, the line where all ceases, the void.

The night swirls around her body and her legs feel funny, so she stands very still in the center of the square roof, the granite pebbles under her feet, gazing out at the high rises and twinkling lights, and out at the tiny cars below spraying water in the cool, cool air.

And then June notices the man with the monocle in a circle of people. And something that is loose shifts inside her. The sides of the building continue to tug and pull from all directions, but something has changed. Something has shifted inside her. The man with the monocle suddenly looks very young and clean. The man with the monocle suddenly looks like even he, who appears on the surface to be so rock hard, could be trampled. He has a beautiful face. It is very white, like a wax face, and his clean skin, his white skin, looks young glistening in the night rain.

He smiles at June.
She smiles back.

He comes up to her. "Are you alright?"

June nods and says something like, "It's not safe over there where everyone's joking around."

"It is safe," he insists, but June knows it is not safe. Nothing is safe feeling the way she feels.

"You'll be alright," he says, but he does not leave. He stays beside June and together they both stand very still while other bodies drift away from them, laughing and talking.

Now that he is there June feels a different pull of gravity on her limbs. It does not replace the pull of the edge, nor does it diminish the feeling. It magnifies it. She puts her hand on his sleeve for balance. He looks so clean. His skin shines. It is his solitude that she is seeing, perhaps his own destitution. But she is unable to say anything. It is most difficult to speak of simple things.

"Let's go back down," he says finally, and she nods and is glad. Her longing has become so strong. His tiny mouth, his beautiful, tiny mouth like a pea pod. Everyone else is already climbing down the fire escape, clambering over the precarious edge, heads then hands disappearing into the night. June feels dizzy. She hands over her martini glass.

"Hold this for me," she says. The sides of the building swerve.

Sitting on the sofa again, the room now muggy, June feels like she is going to cry. And it is all she can do not to cry. She listens to the girl talking about her boss: He was eating breakfast with his lover when she picked up the envelope he wanted her to Fed-Ex, and when she opened it to add the papers it was an image of a man giving a blow-job to a bellhop.

Everywhere people are sloshed. The man with the monocle is across the room in conversation. When he comes over he asks if anything is wrong. Something may be wrong but she does not know what it is, so she shakes her head. She was so happy and now this, she cannot explain it... but because it is a party, and what can you do with this feeling at a party, she can't even articulate it to herself, she must bury it. The man with the monocle hands her another drink.

This is a true story about June, who only wants to exist but is imaginary, though if she were real this is what it would all seem like pretty much, except for the untold parts, like the part about the marble necklace that a girl put around her neck in the bathroom, and years later she would find it in a pocket and remember that night as if it had existed, as if it hadn't all been dreamed up, as if there were a marble necklace and a girl with her heart sewn on her shirt, named June.

They Have a Place for Girls Like Her

If she could have spelled it out letter by letter, at the rubbery lace table, cake leaking blue frosting, ragged paper cup, it would have made a square:

T R Y
H A R
D E R

If she could have pronounced the sum of it when she was this young, having that currency, she would have sworn, "I'm bad now, but one day, you'll see, I'll be good." She would devote her whole life to this effort. She would push forward, out of breath, with an adventurer's abandon. She would persist (grazing the underbelly of sky). She would not stop (oomph, hurled down the highway bloodstream) until she had arrived. Crayons in hand crumbling from determination, wax melting as the paper tore, she drew a darker sun.

Rabbit Hole

girl in pinafore   yellow shirt with Mary Jane collar   hand over mouth   fingers spread   cyan sky   spot of cotton cloud

arms out   floating   feet apart hang on air   green prisms   yellow forest lawn

mouth to mouth   two girls   a dock

white tights   ballet shoes black   stairs unfurl   vertigo   hand reaching out at top of stairs   falling

green water   treading   all alone   clothes bloat   blue hairband mouth open above surface   darkness   tight space

green grass   eyes closed   prone on back

white of boiled egg at cusp of lips   mouth open   white teeth green background   out of focus

fixing white tights   can't pull crotch up   standing   bending over pinafore up   hair over face   forest floor sitting in grass   feet in focus   loves me   loves me not   yellow skirt blooms like petals being plucked in hand   stamen in center 2 petals still attached   tulip   dark setting sky   last sun blooms on lip of skirt   showing white slip

clay teeth   held at crotch   top and bottom jaw   chatter box   blue stitching on hem of blue dress

hair in mouth biting hair   hides all but chin   bottom row of teeth like chatterbox bottom jaw   behind bloom tulips out of focus   fuchsia

rock path   prone on stomach   hands fall onto sides of lawn

mouth open   flossing teeth with hair   cuts across top lip   cyan sky and green slope of hill   face glistens in brilliant sun or flood-lights   eyes closed   can see to darkness in open throat   ecstasy spot of   cotton cloud

dandelions and white flowers must be clover   hands pulling white tights at ankles   tights are too small or coming off   line of trees cling to top   cropped   can see white sky almost rosy in spots

golden grass like hay   white tights in hay grass   legs spread open black ballet shoes

blue hairband   hand grips grass   long hair spills onto grass trees like water   shaky cyan sky   face and hair over face   blue pinafore   running or leaping

dark barn   arms stick in white tights all the way to elbows   eyes closed   head down   face near crotch

soap bar   forcing mouth open   dark in corners   hand gripping arm holding jaw   eyes closed   froth on lips

fly,"
"I want to
said June
softly

Each day June ran in a strict circle around the earth. Laces double knotted, ears plugged and fed to music; a beat, a drone, a high pitch or wave, she ran clockwise to the thump of her heart, always along the same circular path. It is a path trampled out by her feet alone, and while it zigs and zags, its orbit always takes her back to where she started out.

There is something between her and the knotty tree as she passes it, the bikers, the boarded up house, something that keeps her contained, always inside the boat of her own skin. But this motion of the body forward, like a ball of wool tossed repeatedly in the air, begins to loosen (feet landing and landing again) the feeling of being papered behind eyes, behind schemas, diagrams, maps, knots, figures, walls; stuck.

If someone were just up ahead — a truck dumping loads of soil onto this path — June might run a spiral that climbed gradually, truckload-by-truckload, heavenward. But instead, her sneakers etch singing grooves in the mud, dig deeper the trench in the round, flat earth.

Close now to the molten exuda. Close now to the core. And all the blind stars shrieking.

This Small Sound

Her father has a red heart twice the average size, a double cherry. A heart this size is too large for its cage, so the heart is shrinking. Before it was expanding, but now they say it is shrinking. It will always be larger than average. It will always be like those women who lose too much weight all at once and then look tired.

His heart is slamming the blood through a tiny trap door; the door opens and closes, opens and closes with a metal clinking sound. If you saw the heart beating, you would see two patched tears in the ventricles and a metal valve at the aortic mouth. The tears would be healing and the heart would be shrinking, though you would not see this, it would be too slow, but the eight hundred cc's of water around the heart would now be only ten.

Her father thought he might have pulled a muscle under his angel wing but his lung had collapsed. After they used a rubber hammer to find the pool of water, and after they tapped his back with a needle through his ribs, the water came out in two parts: first, one point two; then, point eight. It drained into a plastic bag. The liquid was clear, clear enough to read a newspaper through. If he is able to see past all this, through to the other side, as though reading a newspaper through one point two liters of water, he will be able to start living again, but the metal door will always be clink clinking in his heart.

When it began he was out of breath or his breath was raspy. He was coughing all the time with a dry sort of cough. This was the sound of his heart failing. He would cough a few times and this would be the blood backing up in his heart and the water backing up in his lungs.

The nurse gave him a paper thimble and two white pills, and after that he was drowsy. He looked like a little boy falling asleep and waking to open his eyes suddenly in the middle of bad dreams. Then they wheeled him away, and when they brought him back, he was white with cold, glass skin, and a long piece of tape down the centre of his chest. There was grease on his eyelids and he had a tube in his mouth inflating his chest like a balloon machine. This did not look like breathing. Each time the machine puffed, his whole body shook and then stopped still. There was a tube draining his stomach under the blanket, and a tube in his penis, and a tube in the side of his neck, and tubes in his wrists. Later, with white stubble on his face, he would start to look like a shipwrecked sailor, the ones you see in Saturday afternoon television reruns, but now he didn't look like a sailor, or a father, or like *her* father, or like anyone alive even... and standing there, holding his puffy finger, she wondered where her father was. She thought of how he joked and she tried not to think too much of loving him. The machines made loud buzzing noises, and the red lights flashed, and the blinking numbers continued to drop and suddenly go up.

She had been standing there beside him a long time. It is impossible to say how long because in this intensive care unit there is no night and day, there is only this thin thread of life dipping and shooting back up on the charts. She had been staring at him when, suddenly, he opened his eyes and then closed them, and something in his eyes told her that her father had died as a man but was trying to come back to life as a cyborg. He was trying his best to learn how.

She puts an ear close to his chest and hears the racket. It sounds like a tin hammer punching a coin. It sounds like there could be a factory assembly line in there. It sounds hollow and far away, underwater. It is a sound that frightens her, but she knows she must love the sound. That is the small sound his life now makes.

Later she will follow him, visit that place where baobab trees line the ocean floor and beakless birds dive for worms. She will climb through the little trapdoor and travel through to the other side: drifting down, down, from red at three hundred feet, to green, down to deep, dark brilliant blue, where violet penetrates in spots, far down below, past blue green schools of mackerel and herring, floats of Portuguese men of war, azure tinted wings of swimming snails, below the diatom meadows and drifting sargassum weed, to a place that reveals creatures all crystal clear, transparent hordes of arrow worms, glassworms, comb jellies, the larvae of millions of fish, down farther than the jelly fish medusa, deep brown in hue, where no sunlight reaches, down, down, to the sound of her own heart beating and mile upon mile of elevator muzak.

June's Greatest Day

Today is the greatest day of her life. Today is really the greatest day of her life. Believe June. Believe her, tied to her bed like one tied to a love. June fantastically licks her lips. June is in a fantastic nightmare where she is incredibly dry. Like she has been breathing heavily, feeling her body from the inside, feeling her body from the outside, touched, feeling another body touched, feeling what it is to be a round, physical body and not one drawn with pencils. June is like the Spanish man on TV, crawling through a dusty, painted, desert searching for Agua. He finds a tap sticking out of the ground and, bending up to it on his knees with open mouth, he turns the metal handle propeller and... and nothing flows. This is June so happy to have the very same tap in her room, in her half sleep she is sure she can hear it drip. Reaching out through the slushy morning sounds, reaching, always reaching, this is June's greatest day, her greatest hour, her greatest nightmare, everything she ever hoped for, but such a parched throat.

June is always undone by her own body bending and moving and being a body against objects, a body against others, that she has little room for vowels, syllables. Just now she twists in the sheets — this is June calling out, and sometimes June singing; this is the entire paperback of her day. An entire biography devoted to twenty-four short hours.

... June twists under the white morning sheets. Her right hand is raised: reaching for the tap, asking a question, waving a flag? If only someone would hold her now, momentarily, as though calming down a child, June could learn not to twist, could see the path out of the desiccated expanse, could lie quietly and sleep. This being June's greatest day.

The Chair

From *SWISH*:

the mair has a chair
with long hair the mair
dansis arond the chair and singe
a prity song but he gest
the werds all rong

June's
Tea Party

"The whole world is breaking up," said June, meaning pieces of dust were floating through the light too quickly to catch any, meaning the carpet cleaners were coming that day.

June had seen the sun and moon slip, the sun come and go. She liked to walk the streets, avoiding all thoughts of the future. "The future is for the birds," she said, meaning that the future really didn't exist. Who was she? You know the story of how she drew pictures of yellow birds with trees scratching the page like sharp needles. The pages cracked and split under the branches but June somehow did not fall off, her face staring out, a hinge, saying, "This is what I'm afraid of." June in her gown. June with her crown. June trying to speak, but so quiet only the chair listens.

"Hello," she says to the chair. "It's bright out isn't it!"
(nods the chair)
"If you need me to scratch —"
The chair walks away. It is fine on its own.
"Oh," says June and sits silent again.

And June is alone again wondering what to do, waiting for someone to take her, to leave her, waiting to become responsible for someone to hold her, to lose her, listening to the *tap tap tap* of a typewriter next door, wondering what it all means. Having once read about someone listening to the *clack clack clack* of another typewriter in someone else's story.

"You're back, come in, sit down," she says to the chair. But the chair sways past her down the hallway into the kitchen and puts the kettle on for tea. "Well you don't have to be angry," she says, pouting, afraid to sit down on any surface in case it storms away too.

The man comes into the room wearing his monocle. June does not realize the monocle is meant to intimidate her, which it does. He sits on the chair and the chair moans softly with pleasure. The man stands up and removes his coat, spreading it across the chair's arched back. He sits down again and the chair sways beneath him like a pussycat.

June kicks her toe at the wall thinking, "red tea, green tea, black tea." Then says, "Excuse me," as the Mason jars shake. The chair rocks back and forth, the man stroking the doweled spokes with his long, angular fingers.

"Excuse me," June says to them again, "I think this has gone far enough," but they don't even look up. Picks up the Earl Grey, puts it in the pot and places three mugs on the counter. June stares at the kettle which is now rattling on the element. As the siren wails, the couple topples over, entwined in one another. The centre has been sliding for years and it slides into the tea pot. June stirs in the honey. She likes it sweet. "Sometimes," June thinks, "you believe it's all about a partridge when it's really about race car driving." June stops drawing yellow birds and starts drawing Fords, always green. She only has five colours, red, yellow, blue, green, orange. "Tea's ready," she says.

The man lifts his monocle to his eye and helps the chair to its feet. June steps up to him and puts her palm flat on the middle of his chest. He does not disappear. He does not say anything. The chair winks at him and he smiles back.

June had felt his heart. Fast and steady, it was there beating away. "Gerbils have hearts too," she thought, but his heart was a lot bigger than a gerbil's. She rubbed his shoulders from behind with her hands, and he stood there looking out the window, sipping the hot, honey tea.

June didn't know what to say, and anyway her tongue had shriveled up like a sun-dried apricot. The man spoke finally. "June," he said. But she could only stand there looking at him, her eyes liquid. "Everything tumbles," he said, as if it was some great revelation, then he put on his coat and walked out the front door. June was left with the dishes to wash. The chair looked cross, knowing, perhaps, that she was restricted to the house, wanting so badly to follow the man with the monocle to the end of the street, to the end to the earth — how would you feel stuck in a house, no knowledge, never having studied the question of how to leave?

There was nothing June could do then. It wasn't her fault the man had come, in the first place. He had just arrived like anyone arrives, with a thud, or a shake, or a wail. Just like that, so she couldn't help the chair's pain, though the chair's pain had really surfaced, become molten; red paint was sliding off like blood. Sometimes June wished the chair didn't exist. It just sat around. Men walked in, fucked it, left. The chair sulked, June washed the mugs. June was beginning to tire of it all. "No more birds!" she frowned. "No more goddamn yellow birds!" Her tongue had come back in full, a thick cow's tongue.

What do you do when someone you dream of, though whose name and face you don't know, comes into your kitchen and sits in your favorite chair? Her hands were on the crayons. She grabbed a green one and began to draw. But the cars she drew all sprouted wings. June had forgotten there is yellow in the colour green. The center spiraled out the teapot and into a crack in the floorboards. Later, the carpet cleaners would suck it into their machine.

The cars she had drawn flapped their new wings and flew off out the window. Just June and the chair again. "Just you and me," said June to the chair. The chair didn't answer. June sat facing the window wondering what the bells were ringing for. The brightness made her squint.

It's a Rain

It's a rain of black pearls, constellations, the Morse code. Blood unchecked, she bleeds a train, an ocean wall. Waiting to surface, she's not breathing, just bleeding — there are tendrils, roots, threads, some hair, strings of pus, but mostly she's bleeding and she's bleeding bad; origami swans, cells, the sun, baths of honey, black velvet sunsets, a Klezmer band, her mother's coat. She's bleeding roses by the dozen. She's been bleeding all month and tomorrow she'll still be bleeding, a dark red kiss, stuffed zebras, blood oranges, phosphorescence. Ratty skivvies stained with gorgeous mistakes, she put the x's and o's in all the wrong places. It's happened so many times it's an abstract drawing. If you bleed hard enough you colour the world. Up to her waist in cranberry, there's junk floating around — an old piano, even a few toy boats, she's bleeding out, jampots of colour; maroons, russets, burgundies. The doctors say it's normal, not to worry, bleeding jellyfish medusa, a flute that once belonged to her sister. She should have known there was a space inside, a kind of depot for lost things, picket lines and parades, a phalanx of moths, sex-on-wheels shows. It brings on this rain of pearls, constellations, Braille. It's a rain hard as a hockey player. It howls loud the way a tunnel is deep. It's not a storm you would want to be barefoot in. And when the odd piece of wood slips out, she sets it aside, for a raft.

Water Had Walls Then

June is hunched in a ball. Her body is rolled and round as if to force strong thoughts (that will multiply and then pour out her eyes when she looks at you). June does not look at anyone these days. People think she's cross but she is only preoccupied, as if she were in the middle of a very complicated math calculation. Today she is sitting just beside the kitchen mat, head down, like wrapping herself up as one might wrap a gift, although there are no ribbons, and the paper is only the shell of herself which wants to curl off. Maybe this is what she waits for, June, for that shell to crinkle and peel and then, June wonders, will she be old?

Kit cat jumps on the kitchen window ledge. June looks back into the green Siamese eyes that hold you like a pounce.

June is a body in the wind. June is a body about to peel. June is a body that has struck-out. June is a body the colour of a ripe peach and her spine arcs.

June stretches her neck and lights a pipe with her long white fingers. Her hands shake. She cannot fight the winds that blow around her kitchen.

Sometimes June talks to her pots hanging on the wall above the stove, brass, gleaming. Sometimes she wears a pot on her head, as if she were going to the trenches, and the bullets fly all around her. June likes to pretend she is a man, wearing a pot on her head, smoking a pipe, doing chin-ups until the blood cracks into the skin of her face.

It is late night, several days earlier. June and her friend, Hillary, crawl into bed with a boy. Really, it is more like they both circle around him centripetally, slowly pulled together into his gravity-centered chest.

On the earth there is a thick atmosphere, unlike the moon.

Walking into the chilly room, his door left ajar, they go toward separate sides of the bed. From his languorous pose, he looks at them both in surprise. Cruelly, he makes no remark or movement, but watches as they hesitate, blunder. June closes the door behind her. The moment they let go of each other's hand and step away, is when that night threatens most.

"His skin's soft, isn't it, June?" June brushes over his chest and shoulders with her lips. *Yes, his skin is soft.* He lies back in the middle of the bed with his hands behind his head and closes his eyes. They begin to chat with each other about the boy, laughing, as if he were not, in fact, right there between them. Each is focused on one side: thigh, nipple, lobe of ear. June does not have to avert her eyes because, although the moon is out like a crisp clear bonnet, the curtains save her. The two kiss his mouth separately, one at a time, taking turns, a pendulum swinging back and forth. He touches them in a calculated, careful way. Somehow, something is missing. "How are you doing, June?" asks Hillary. June is doing many things but does not answer how. His sex is a nest of hungry, baby birds. The boy bites June on her shoulder and growls. He turns to bite Hillary and they lock eyes and then he pulls Hillary on top of him. His hand holding June's loosens.

June walked into the bedroom trembling, but now she is only following a script. The bed holds all three but barely, this much has become clear; a triangle is not a good circle. The boy doesn't speak much, only to answer in staccato, and later, he will smoke a cigarette by the fire burning to ash.

From across the pillows, Hillary. Says, "Hello."

June has to squint — a piercing star — is dizzy, it is — it is — as if she looked out into the night in the darkest hour of winter — and light streamed in. She is blind. She is blinded by a single star, light years away. The boy, a magnet between them, now forcing June and Hillary further and further apart, and making the whole bed spin as if it might take off at any cough or sneeze, hurling them each in a different direction into the atmosphere. Emotions are so precise in this closed room, but no one is able yet to define what it is they are feeling. All June knows is the taste of salt and the *tick tick tick* of the clock.

Later he says, "This is why I didn't want to play," because things have gone a little off and no one quite knows how to climb back up to that height. Hanging from toes and fingertips — luckily June has been doing chin-ups. She has no trouble just hanging on, suspended for a while; her muscles like lumps in the throat.

The next morning he tells them about the *cabane à sucre* where he worked for a weekend with beer as pay, tapping all the bleeding maples with buckets and metal taps. How the tree sap begins to run in the spring with the first thaw. How the sap is collected in buckets, but not too much or the tree dies. June feeling her two feet under the breakfast table.

June inhales the pipe smoke and it seems to give her more substance; her spine straightens out a little. The Siamese is arching like a bow in the window, and then June is flattening again, into the wood of the floor, no pot lid on her head to dispel the shrapnel, bending into the planks as if this hard pillow might cushion the fall. Her movements are generous as though she has been straining under a blood sun, and she is fluid the way that kind of movement places you at the top of any mountain. In the kitchen, quiet and quite still except for the occasional breath, she is a swimmer, winding her body through the sand and dusty winds that ripple over her way from the horizon.

When White is Placed Next to Snow

I

Oranges are not important. What is important is not the heat. What is important does not taste important. What is important cannot be measured with ruler or string.

Apology is important; it is close to tears, though not in vogue.

II

Look at June's friend, Bill, carrying his floor in his arms. Bill has what is important. He is building a new wood floor. When the floor is ready he'll gather some accordion players off the street and they'll play on it. Dance on it. Harmonize on it. Drink all night long and party on it. Bill bundles the planks with string and carries the bundle by the string handle he's attached. He loves carrying the wood in his hand like a suitcase, laying out the boards, when he feels the urge, to sell lemonade. One day he wants to take up the square stage and construct a long, narrow, wooden path that will stretch all the way, past the last lawn in the city, to the sea.

III

In her dream, the prime minister has a unicorn machine on top of his car. Not wanting to be uncool, the prime minister tells the people that unicorn machines really *are* in fashion. He is partly embarrassed by the unicorn machine and trying to make up for the fact of it. There is something about a unicorn machine that is very important which the prime minister does not understand — can never understand. But June understands what is important about a unicorn machine.

IV

In another dream, October and grape jelly are the colour of memory. This is not that important.

Today the colour WHITE is important. White is lonely when placed next to snow.

(Look at how small white has become)

white

June Makes a Friend

(a fable of desire)

"A cone form, then squeeze it back into a cake shape," June is thinking, but the wet clay between her hands will not center and hush. "Hello?" she says, lifting her foot off the pedal. The room is still, but somewhere someone is trying to sing — a piano perhaps, a piano or choir? The slip slipping between her fingers, oozing like a cream and drying into tight cracked gloves. But there it is again, a single note held strong. With a sigh, the cylinder in her hands gurgles and folds.

"Would you mind cutting me loose?" a voice says. June picks up her wire and slices twice underneath.

"Cut it loose and begin again," thinks June, always hovering on the brink of a bridge to anything just barely beginning.

"Please. A little to the left," says a voice. She begins a gentle massage. June's clothes, covered in splashes of slip drying, eyes focused on the center of another world.

"To the left a little more," thinks June, rubbing the clay.

"A little more," she rubs the clay smooth. "Ahhh," says the voice, "Thanks. That's the spot!"

"You're welcome," says June, and she continues to rub smooth the wet form in her hands, up and down, up and down, with wet warm thumbs, up and down, so that there are no creases or dents or bumps but instead a growing hollow shape stretching and reaching with long motions up — up — up —

"So good," says the voice smiling at June. "So much better. Awfully cramped before. Tight and cramped. You can't even imagine!"

"Poor darling," says June, cooing.

"I wouldn't mind a little more hair," says the voice. "And make it curl."

"Pushy pushy," she mutters, reaching for a pick to scratch his head. He moans and leans into the massage. "Don't stop. Don't ever stop," he says breathlessly, eyes closed. She runs the pick in jagged lines over his scalp, creating a long mane. She blows off sticky bits of excess clay. "If only..." says the voice and June says, "If only..." and they gaze at each other silent and still in the room heavy with dust.

"You've become something else," says June wrinkling her brow. "You've become. Yes, you've become much more. A boy."

"A ceramic boy!"

"Yes," says June.

"There are greater failures," says the boy with an air of erudition. Busy with her pick, she does not answer.

June is hunched low, absorbed and intent on something outside herself. Sitting on the wooden bench three floors below ground level, shaping with her two thumbs, June is in a pure state, a state of grace. "What an odd thing a boy is. What funny knobbly legs you have and crooked back. I'll give you some clothes."

"You're no princess yourself," says the boy defensively. No, June is certainly not a princess, though this many feet below ground she may well be in a dungeon.

"A ceramic boy. My own ceramic boy," she says emphatically.

"And you. You're not a boy. What are you?"

"June," says June quietly, breathing out with a rush of air.

"My June," says the boy.

"My boy," says June.

"Yes," says the boy.

"Yes," says June.

He interrupts with a new thought. "But... but, I'm only what you make of me. You like me now. But if you should decide you hated me, I would be no more than a voice again. Not even that. I would be no more than a lump of — a lump of —"

"Nothing," says June in the quiet room while she fashions a jacket.

"You would be my executioner," says the boy.

"Do you like your new coat?"

"Very much. I have never had a coat before."

"You've never had anything before."

"How sad," says the boy.

"No," says June. "That is the way we all begin."

"You're right. I had forgotten." June runs her fingers through his dark hair.

"But," says the boy jumping up, excited, "if you should love me... with all your heart, I mean, really love me, I'd be very precious. Others would desire me too. They would covet me. They'd pay to own a work of art like me, might even fight wars one day over me."

"True."

"I'm nothing without your love... do you love me, June?" June stares at the boy and the boy stares at June and the wide expanse becomes just a tiny bit smaller.

"Where I lived before," says the boy sadly, "there were only balconies. No stairs. Just balconies. There weren't even any ladders. We used fishing rods a lot, of course. We had no choice. But it is better to be here now on a lower level, with you."

"Sweet pea," says June.

"June," he says, clearing his throat. "What I'm trying to say is, I'm not what I once was. You would not recognize me if you saw me on those balconies before," and the boy laughs wickedly and his eyes glitter like dark wet capers.

"Do you like your coat?"

"I said I did."

"True," says June.

"I am nothing like I was before. I was never this tamed," he says loudly. June has given the boy some trousers and shoes and a belt with a big buckle. The belt buckle is the finishing touch.

"You are lovely. Perfect," says June. "My peach." June rummages in her tool bag for a tool to sign her name.

"Yes, I am quite changed," he says. But June does not respond. "I SAID, I AM QUITE CHANGED." He reaches suddenly for his curly front locks and squeezes them into two pointy horns. He tears the belt from his pants and attaches it as a tail. Scratching his horns, "Itchy," he murmurs.

June looks up from her tools, "What have you done!" A growl comes from the boy. He trembles and then the trembling finishes. "Hello, June. Nice to see you again, puss."

"Oh!" says June, hand to her mouth. "It's you!"

"What a quick wit you are! Thought you had done away with me forever?" he asks in a deep voice.

"You don't frighten me," says June, grabbing hold of him tightly with a fist.

"No? Don't I have you burning?" June stares at him, wildly, wondering what to do with the creation she loves. "You needn't answer. I can still read your mind."

"You bore me," says a quite brave (and trembling) June.

"Bore you!" he laughs, "Oh, pussy cat, let's not play the same tired old games. I'm the only one who *doesn't* bore you. The only one who keeps you sane."

"It's over," she says.

"I think, rather, it's only just begun."

"Go away!"

"Now, now, let's not get testy, puss. Is that all you can think of to say after such time apart? Tsk, tsk. Not very nice. Not very nice at all. And here you are looking so lovely. Mmmm..." he says as saliva spills from his lips.

"Go away," whispers June. "Everything's changed. Go away."

"Not so fast, sweetie," he whispers back fiercely. "You need me! We're accomplices, after all. Think of the destruction we've wrought together. An eternal bond." June remains silent. The clay dust rises in puffs around her. "Bend my way, puss. Bend a little further my way. You love so to be bad. What a delight it is when you wiggle that naughty nose! How it hurts me to see you suffering like this all sugar-coated and sweet!" His laugh echoes off the walls and the brittle clay vessels rock on their shelves.

"Tomorrow I will make you a friend. Because I think you are not really wicked. You are just lonely and bored," says June.

"Oh, come now... sweets!"

"Yes, I'll put you back here on this high shelf here, where you'll be safe," she says standing up. "And tomorrow when you've dried out, I'll make you a friend," says June stiffly. She reaches for the plastic wrap.

"How coy! You're too much! A playmate!" he scoffs with a snap of his sharp tail. It lashes out and, like an arrowhead, tears into June's skin. Blood runs from her arm. Blood runs all over her shirt. The sheet of plastic floats to the floor.

"Naughty man! Naughty man!" she screams as he slips from her grasp. He falls and smacks the whirling wheel, and is flung onto the cement floor. His small, nimble body writhes in protest, kicking and screaming, trying to rock out of its position like a turtle on its back.

"Pussy bitch!" he is yelling.

"Come here, my love," says June, quietly, reaching down and rolling him into a ball. She kneads and flattens and kneads and flattens, smoothing the ball with the heel of her hands. Blood runs from her arm into the clay, moistening it. She kneads with her body's momentum. She begins rubbing out creases and bumps.

A small voice comes from the clay, “A little to the left please, if you will.”

June approaches the bridge to the beginning again. “Hush,” she whispers.

“Where I come from there are only balconies,” says the voice.

“Yes, my love, hush,” says June.

“There are only balconies and we have to catch the rain that falls from the sky with our mouths.”

“Yes, Sweet pea,” she says, molding the clay and smoothing the lumps and creases and imperfections.

“I think you’ve forgotten my hair.”

“So I have,” she says, combing a short brush cut. “There you are.”

“I am very beautiful now,” says the soft voice, touching its face delicately.

“Yes,” says June.

“You have made me,” says the voice, “perfectly.”

“Thank you,” she says, touching up his trousers and leaving him without a belt.

“Where I come from —”

“Yes,” she says, wrapping him in thick plastic so that he will dry slowly and will not crack.

“Where I come from —”

“Yes,” she says, putting him on the high ceramic shelf to be fired in the kiln, and kissing him goodnight on his wet, clay lips.

The Lines of Her Hand

Home:
But she needed only the walls around her like tin can crosses, she needed only her cloth body and its beating tambourine heart.

ABC:
First you take three small stones, and after you swallow them (a, b, c) you will be just that much closer to the ground.

South-south-east:
South-south-east said the sign: so she went. There were stairs. It was chilly. There was grass and a few trees. There were clouds in the sky. It looked a lot like *south-south-west.*

Plug:
Hard round, June with a plug up her nose after a punch, another hard round in the ring, bell dinging.

Key:
The key around her neck on a string: an albatross? a funeral? a wishbone? All the same, it is made of sugar. Sucking on it leaves lace blue stains.

Adventuress:
She skins the chicken, drinks its blood, hatchet on the kitchen counter, blade sharp and gleaming. June, an adventuress in her kitchen, all the wide-eyed pots cheering for her.

Hands:
Two hands in the air, not one — one would be waving a flag, reaching, asking a question. Two is surrender.

Threat:
Tie her down, wrap wire around and around, spread her legs, shoving them apart. Her lips are your lips. Electric chair, there is no emotion. Your hands are rubbing her legs. Electric. Red. There is no need for emotion. Blindfolded, knees stick in her face, she gasps, your hands push her back, an invitation, her paint is slick, cold, there is no need for emotion, upturned duck-bill nose, she is a flirt, the wire cuts her, there's a small piece of muslin fiberfill that's come undone, your hand holds her throat, she moans, there is no emotion, there is no emotion.

Ear:
To have an ear pressed to the floor. To shut out half the noise — cut it equally in half as if a pie. But the math isn't quite right, there would only be distortion. An impoverishment, not a lessening. An ear to the floor would still be a strong funnel.

Locusts:
They landed in a cloud on the lawn, and she was in the bath blowing bubbles when she saw it arrive, a grey dust screaming.

Brush:
A hairbrush makes June a fabulous heroine, in her hand at the day's end like a lit-up torch.

Paring:
The act of cutting away an edge or surface. For most, a paring knife is but a kitchen tool. But look closely at June's arms, at the marks there, razor thin white lines like the lines between lips. Paring: The act of cutting away an edge or surface.

Married:
How do they do it, the ones in black – poor little vaginas puckered towards heaven...

Good:
In the hallway at midnight, the chair is gorging on some bone left to waste. Looks up at June, lip curls. Face of a wicked six - year-old.

Miss:
Doesn't matter if she doesn't miss. If she doesn't miss, it means she isn't jealous of kissing.

Music:
Red violin like her red chair, stained from so much bleeding. June strikes up the bow and what noise! Like cats fucking.

Reply:
Checks the mail slot for anything tiny stuck. Maybe a message the size of a paper cut saying she has just won the lottery. Congratulations!

Dazzles:
String of bright lights dazzling the eyes and June blinks again — the lights — so intense there are tears. June blinking and now wiping her eyes frequently. *Those damn lights, damn strong lights to make her feel like crying.*

Yard:
Things have been left there, odd forms with wood sticking out and pieces of metal, pipes hanging by wires, broken bits of glass strung out on string, or strung on elastic bands, and strings, and some rubber tires. There are piles of old carpet. There is some dirt; there is sand in piles. There are places to hide but not in the piles made of sand. Maybe behind the piles, or maybe behind the tires, or maybe inside the tires, or maybe behind the thing with the pieces sticking out of it, the pieces of metal with rubber strips, or that thing made of sticks.

One Day She Asked a Question

When June was small she wouldn't speak. She learned to read instead. Language came in through the eyes, not out of the mouth. In books words existed on their own, possessing a will and a life of their own.

One day, in a canoe, she asked a question. She was surprised at the question, the sound of her voice. It felt like a bomb but it landed like a petal. Dipped the blade into the thick surface of the cold black lake.

She is trying to figure out what the child knows and what the adult knows. Only able to fall asleep with a doll or a rolled towel in her arms.

June has just woken up and wants to draw the man in her dream. It does not flush away the way other dreams do; it hinges itself inside, like the video she watched of an autopsy. In the video, a young, very pretty lady is shaved to show the deep cuts in her scalp. These look like pale mouths, and with a metal instrument, the coroner probes to measure their depth. In the video the lady lies naked on a table. In June's dream the man floats towards her out of the darkness with an amputated leg. Where the leg is severed — around the white of femur — is his swollen red flesh. It will be a red drawing.

Mistake the ugly for the beautiful. Sleep with the old architect. Kiss the void of his mouth. Steal his loneliness, his quiet depression, his derelict years. He's an insomniac poet. He makes songs out of rope, out of flags, and binds them together with numbers. He sits in an easy chair whittling a bird out of a leaky Bic pen.

But perhaps June cannot go all the way with her exercise. His "bum leg" is red and chaffed, wrapped always in a bandage. "No circulation," he says. As a boy he was kicked in the groin by a horse — this leads to other complications.

He says with tenderness, "You'll age well. You will be a beautiful older woman."

Walk away with indifference. Watch, without feeling a thing, as his eyes bruise. Hunt down the glamour of the city in dimly lit bars, and dilapidated theatres that play organ music. Cling to the smoke exhaled by taxi drivers, as it is the only buttress to another human being. Sleep against a wall sheltered from the sea.

moon, muffler, apocalypse, thighs hot, seared tuna, and then... can't remember the film — oh, a murder, I don't take the bus, fuck you, like hello, five dollars, no rain, I don't have a dog — my boyfriend has a dog, package of cigarettes, tournament, Japanese trees, who's going, a hundred canaries that they're raising out there, an idiotic thing to do — give someone your credit card, it's hardly legal

Her friend Hillary's grandfather had lung cancer. He never smoked, but his wife (her grandma) did. "THAT'S LOVE!" Hillary said.

Now the architect wants to shake her tiny hand. She pulls away, greasy from egg roll snacks. He says with innuendo, "That's okay. Oil's good." But the thought of his hand repels her almost as much as his very thin lips.

When she hides (in another dream) his ankles walk by her face.

Then, in the park, June sees: the tree trunk. The bark has boiled over in the most amazing protrusions, peeling husks, gross deformed knobs, dark oozing scars. In a medical textbook this would be the Elephant Man. Hillary gasps, "Oh! What lovely diseases!" Has mistaken day for night. Has mistaken the ugly for the beautiful again.

This Tastiness Cannot Be Carried

I'm not holding my breath for him,
she said,
first I'll buy a vibrator
and a fish,

now she's really lying, she's telling everyone she's 27. it makes them comfortable. learning things but not what she'd fantasized about. death, is that normal. she wants to make things with plastic flowers, real are cheaper. how would you ask the question

I long

with the bottle of champagne in her arms she couldn't stop crying.

have a baby then you'll feel better. or a small alphabet. or fight a war, then you'll feel better. Patrick's HIV positive. or listen to the moans of buses, windows
no perfume

the girl with the red bicycle

something hard or billy goat style, maybe with some brass or whipped green, or the way honey runs, or hips run behind breath, or the way you can't bruise a river. or a stone.

hard fucked, long hard fucked

confidence
of creating
deliciousness:
this tastiness
cannot
be carried
even by
both hands

must be magic. he's in love with

The Reverse Side of the Letter A:

"The reverse side of the letter A *has always fascinated me."*
— Jim Melchert

(part a)

There was a box. Not a voice box, though the chair did have a soft, buttery voice. A secret box.

C'est nous, ici, la chaise, la chaise rouge. Ahhhh...

...begins the red chair, *(It's us, over here...)*

"I'll take that old chair," says June at the estate sale. The basement is sucking the summer in. It's time to get out of there. She hands over some bills. Red chair slants a little to the left, its black lashes flashing.

— My mother passed away 4 days after my birthday, a woman is saying.

— Oh happy birthday! says another voice.

What is the opposite of flowers, thinks June. She is dreaming of roots and troughs of milk, trying to weigh the difference between lead and gold leaf. She is thinking of glass ornamental grapes, polyester, tacky ashtray stands...

— The yellow zone is for loading and unloading only, says the man directing operations.

— Uh, I wanted to take one more look, I saw a cup —

The man picks up the chair for her and walks outside with it. June moves over to a table of flatware.

what do you believe in,

he is saying as he carries the chair to the car,

what is it about death that scares you,

he shifts the chair to the side of his waist while he opens the trunk; eyelashes flicker as he places the chair down,

why are you afraid of getting older —

are your brown eyes French...

(part b)

Act 1

It is almost the lip of a new day. The red chair is alone in the corner. Only the sound of a grandfather clock suggests signs of activity. Illuminated by the floodlights of a theatrical moon, June's bed is neatly made up, the pillows fluffed and top sheet neatly folded over. The hallway yawns a lion's yawn, when it is suddenly as though the chair, a foot away from June's desk, shifts slightly. Yes... it appears as though the chair is straining.

Does it stretch over towards the desk, upon which lies a leather toolbox and some materials, or is that the moonlight casting strange shadows? Perhaps it is only a matter of a bothersome screw that has come loose again.

seed moon
hate moon
dyad moon
mead moon
wort moon,
barley moon
blood moon
snow moon
oak moon
wolf moon
storm moon
chaste moon

Act 2

Early morning. The razor edge of night has sliced clean through, shades of grey lisp thinly into colour. It is clear, now, that the red chair *was* indeed straining: it sits at the desk working. With a hammer and some wire, it bangs away at two large wheels, attaching them to its front legs. First it wobbles off balance, then it starts rolling around the bedroom, a makeshift wheelchair, knocking over plants, crashing into furniture, leaving long scratches along the walls. As the chair gains control and is better able to navigate, it wheels through the bedroom door, down the hallway, lurching and skidding to stop suddenly, or spin in now delicate, perfect circles. Down the narrow hallway it rolls and finally, over into the kitchen, *bump bump over the hump*. It sits there for a long time directly in front of the sink cabinet.

For many minutes the chair waits, as if at attention. As a swell of light warms the kitchen, the lemon-coloured walls blush as though on fire, sunlight pours from the tap. With a faint *creeak* the low cabinet door swings open. And there, tucked behind the rags, by the detergents and a jar of bacon grease, is a brown paper bag — there's no point taking chances, the bag has been expertly hidden. Inside this bag is a box, which is, in itself, pretty unremarkable; cardboard, a throwaway, like a shoebox, though much smaller. You could fit it into your pocket.

Like a child who collects, from the world around her, her own unique cabinet of curiosities, special rocks, a bird's wing, some old coins, bottlecaps and string, this box also holds a most precious and unusual specimen. It is more than a simple list of treasures; it is a small plastic virgin membrane.

Not a voice box, a secret box.

> **Instructions**: *Inside you will find a colourless, transparent outer wrapper with some red powder inside. The device may be folded up to form a plug. It will also kill bacteria and eliminate infections. It is safe and reliable. It will not stain furniture or clothing. Once inserted, it will dissolve into an adhesive substance that will proceed to seal up. When the male enters, spreading apart the sealed edges, the blood-coloured ingredients release to quickly mix with natural fluids, creating a liquid that resembles blood. If the device does not break on its own, one may discreetly use one's own hands to break it open. Afterwards it may be washed and dried and, once more powder has been added, it may be reused at a later date.*

Listen now (can hear a faint, French whisper alongside the song birds):

... we know too much, we are not cute, we know too much, we know too much, the men in the town, they want to liquor us up, our pretty eyes, our gymnast legs, we play them along like suckers, breaking old man dicks, we are too ancient for that game, need a little one, a new one, a barely started one, need just some bud on the end of a stick

At the Bar

There was a Stan Getz album playing a Stan Getz tune and June, *oh what a feeling*, and June, *oh what a feeling*, and there were people suffering dying in the world too, yes, but there were also people suffering living, loving suffering living.

Arms pale after pale winter.

Life is formed. Organic matter bonds to inorganic matter. RNA creates moulds from DNA chains and collects compounds to fit the moulds.

A Stan Getz album was playing as if it had always been playing and there was smoke as if there would always be smoke.

In nature random patterns are not, in fact, random, but may be plotted on graphs and predicted like the weather. The movement of traffic is no different from the flow of molecules of water from a tap.

Under the noise of the bar crowd.

If these patterns are mapped, plotting: $x = 3a+1$, they produce symmetrical designs: clam shells, mollusks.... On the graph a clam-shaped shell will appear and then another clam-shaped shell, and then another. Or, a mollusk shape will appear and then another mollusk shape, and so on. Nature loves symmetry.

They had a feverish love for the world that day that would not go away.

The universe is finite but without end. If you reach the end you come back to where you began. Home. Back to the same point, though at a different point in time.

Let me help you off with your golden chains, we'll throw them in the river. He hadn't had dinner. He said he was getting drunk.

Armenian orange, chestnut, pineapple, banana bunt, cupcakes, Bishop's cakes, foam cakes, cheesecakes. *Did I meet you before,* she said, *Are you the man I met baking castles out of cookie dough?*

The barmaid came to settle.

As she left for the washroom, June overheard: *virgule, violet*

The Three Sisters

The soft swallow enters the room, reverberates off the walls. The soft swallow and the clock ticking. In an empty kitchen, the bubble gulps of the drain and the dripping of the tap. *Plip, plip, plip. Plip,*

plop,

plop.

A lot has been happening lately, some of which you know about. June's crayons crumbled in pieces in the cardboard Crayola box, and then they all melted during the fire — a river of wax. She is now burning the rest of it, pastels and primaries, prints and solids, fuscias, mauves, russets, aquas... stoking the fire in her underwear. The colour has finally begun to hush, though the music is so loud you couldn't hear the fire anyway if it chose to roar suddenly like a need bursting out.

June feels like she is inside a punching bag with no zipper. *Like being rolled under logs and then having to perform for an audience of people who are thick and hate flat ones*. But then, June has always assumed it is just this way for everyone, being on stage in a strange poem.

She wonders if it is really possible. All those nightmares in which she is pregnant, running away from the delivery room, newly expectant, or breastfeeding triplets... the same feeling now, that she has been ambushed, her body not her own. The man with the monocle tells her, "We're often attracted to what's wrong for us." He is always reasonable. She throws her favorite sweater on the fire.

Pieces of the bleak winter sky begin falling and the branches outside the window turn white. She remembers climbing those summer treetops in homemade jumpers, with skinned knees. She remembers the taste of her own blood. She remembers the boy with the binoculars across the street watching her undress at night. *Is anyone out there watching now*, she wonders. She walks out onto the front porch. Like icing sugar, the snow has left everything clean, coating over all the ugliness, making everything appear new again.

June walks along the sidewalk, picturing the recipe in the big cookbook. There is a soft haze almost like breath around her body. Pools of water appear where her bare feet leave the ground. June questions: *What does it mean exactly, to be blue, to wear white on the outside, to have red run from inside, to cut a yellow pineapple and then bake it?*

She had wanted to call this guy up. To call him up might at least make him flinch, struggling to find her name, "Um — um — June!" And then to say, because of course he wasn't the least bit worried, but to say, "I just wanted you to know... I'm late." But she decided to celebrate instead. She decided to make a pineapple upside-down cake: turn everything upside down that wasn't right side up.

Plip, plip, plip goes the tap as she mixes. White flour rises and falls like smoke. June feels like punching and holding at the same time. She worries that she is beginning to go deaf from listening to too-loud music.

The rules of the game are the following: The three large sisters must find the three fishermen brothers and, after killing them, replace them in their jobs and daily routine without anyone suspecting or realizing this has happened. The three sisters will abandon their own jobs at the cannery, stepping invisibly into the coveralls and slickers that the men wear each day to fish.

The first sister spots Brother Number 1. She slices a sharp lid at his neck from a can of albacore tuna, hoping to cut his jugular, but she misses and the lid rolls down the hill. The other sisters try poisons and open pits, they sabotage fishing boats that the men will step into, but nothing works, and the three sisters begin to suspect that the men know they are being followed. They begin to fear that the men will retaliate. The second sister starts biting her nails and the first sister starts knotting her hair when the brothers pass in town.

The three sisters wear large apron-like dresses over their ample frames. The brothers fish together and talk on the wharf about interest rates and boats. Because it is two groups of triplets it is really one against one, not three against three. The large sister trio never succeeds in snuffing out and effacing the men, though they continue to plot, and now fear the brothers. The men will never know the sisters exist except to see right past them when they pass one another in town. The sisters do not know they are (and will always be) safe, completely, boringly safe. The men do not realize they are in grave danger.

The timer rings. Out it comes. Sweet pineapple upside-down cake, upside down until June flips it. It is there, level, perfectly round and intact, brown sugar dripping onto the plate and the pineapples like gold bracelets, five in all — topped with cherries.

A triumph. June breaks off a piece of cake and has to put it down for a moment. It is too hot. She licks the stickiness from her hand in anticipation; somewhere inside, a shiny, waxed paper coin hides... whirling.

To any loose man

to:

any loose man came over and looked in her eyes, wearing the neon pussy medallion, and she with her manners mummy taught, lunging and thrusting at some vague long way off, trying to scoop up the night and have it last forever in a conversation or a large glass of beer

are you still going after more? are you still going after money, status, praise? are you still going after friendship? are you going after love?

it's a long way off, and hard to cool down, and not necessarily better than comfort

in Israel they're building a bridge 2 inches under so you can walk on water. also a way to cool off

Behind the Monocle

The man with the monocle had his house, three floors high and near a woodpile, and all the summer lupins and daffodils knew his name — a name with CAPITALS, the name burned on the wood sign. He was a man who drank whisky, a man who liked chopping wood and clearing his driveway of snow. He was a man, with a gold-rimmed monocle that he held up to his squint eye and peered through, and hummed, and you could see the eye like a telescoped worm shifting, and it made June feel put in her place when he looked at her like that. That was the kind of man he was.

June was alone in his library. A man with business to do, he would be late returning.

June had been unable to drum up a flashlight or candles during the storm that began after he left, but she had found a curious thing. Earlier that afternoon, in the fruit bowl, lodged between a banana and a pear, she had discovered his monocle. She noticed, looking through it, that it seemed to make a thing brighter. At first, peering through made everything blur, but then, if she didn't shift her focus but continued staring straight ahead, whatever she looked at began to shine. She slipped the monocle into her pocket.

When the lights flickered and died, June curled up on the sofa in the pitch dark and felt something hard press against her leg. She pulled out the monocle. Taking it and lifting the glass to her eye, she found that she could see again. Focusing through the monocle on an isolated thing, like a pen, or a coin or her hand, she could see perfectly as though using a small flashlight.

The rain whistled against the windowpanes and shook the man's house. She knew it would be a long time before he returned.

What June does in the dark:

What June does in the dark is take the book from the shelf, a book with a thin spine that she had noticed earlier. It is a small book, the size of her hand, and the leather is worn and soft. When she opens the book, she finds that it is a book she has written herself. And, with the help of the monocle, she begins to read.

For a while June is not sure whether she loves or hates the book. She is compelled, certainly. She is fascinated – her heart beats quickly, her palms are moist as she hunches into the book's pages. She continues reading without once looking up. But she is not sure whether she loves or hates the book.

Seeing it written was learning that all was not solid, but transparent: *desk, cupboard, sentence, heart, kettle, face, promise, rock, time.*

It was a small book, but it was also dense, and she was there well into the evening, reading.

When the man returned he found June in a state. It was as though a ghost had passed through her.

At first he had to calm her down, and then he tried to make sense of it, and then, when he finally saw the book, he threw back his head and laughed. "June, June... every woman fears the same thing," and he poured her a stiff drink. He knew numbers well, he told her, and the numbers would work out for her.

But he hadn't seen the book. No, he couldn't begin to understand her feeling of utter helplessness (that death could overtake her, that motherhood could snare her), didn't know what was inside those pages: weapons, the way a butter knife can carve out a heart or a tongue, the way a skipping rope could hang a dog from a tree. Numbers papered the walls of his three-story house (a story for each ex-wife). He had worked out the math. June would be fine.

June took his monocle and ran.

She raced past the long line of pine trees at the end of his driveway. She ran past the swamp where bulrushes grew in summer. She continued running, dodging branches and jumping rocks, until she was deep into the forest.

She stopped. Breathing heavily, she started to look around. The rain had let up. There was the sound of foliage dripping on the forest floor. She took the monocle from her pocket and lifted that gold-rimmed circle to her eye. Gazing through, she could see from his perspective, knowing absolutes and doubting nothing, the way numbers always work themselves out with straight fraction lines or fixed decimal points. For once she could see clearly, through to the spliced core.

Holding the monocle up to the rough bark of a tree, she could see there, diving valleys, ridges, rivers and streams, misty mountain-tops, meadows, a vast, bucolic landscape spanning miles and miles, undulating and pitching between shadow and light.

In the ground moss, kneeling, she saw glowing neon, gardens, the countryside, hedges, colonnades, cottages, archeological sites, pastures. In the thick bed of pine needles she saw again, a microcosm of life, a world teeming with it: cities reduced to a mass, public places, temples, the figures of power and history, platforms, high-rises, skateboarders and skyscrapers, everything inextricably bound together yet delineated by soft and hard edges, light and darkness. The monocle grew hot in her grip. Behind the glass June *could see, could see...* bush fires starting up, *could see...* small blazes everywhere. And there was the man, she knew, somewhere, far away, squinting, waving his arms by his A-Frame, calling her back. He seemed just old then, and half mad with the texts of numbers flattening him, calling for her to come home... yelling, "11:46! 11:47! 11:48!"

She loved him then. It was a small realization, but she knew she loved him. If she had been born with dragon breath *that could fire this easy...* If she had been born with Superman eyes *that could see this clear...* June was aiming to burn through it all the way only a man or a god can, when the ground caught fire under her feet. The soles of her shoes warmed, then caught fire too. It felt good for a moment, as though the heat was inside, plunging outwards from her heart. Then it burned. She began to jump up and down.

"11:55! 11:56! June – come home!" bellowed the man at the top of his lungs.

If he could have seen her then, deep in the forest, it might have looked like she was practicing a strange dance, flailing her arms, hopping in circles, with swift, jerky strides.

Red the most

The lines of the graph plot the contraction of muscles of the hand and forearm under the influence of various coloured lights which, according to Charles Féré, can be felt even with the eyes closed. Violet has the least effect, red the most.

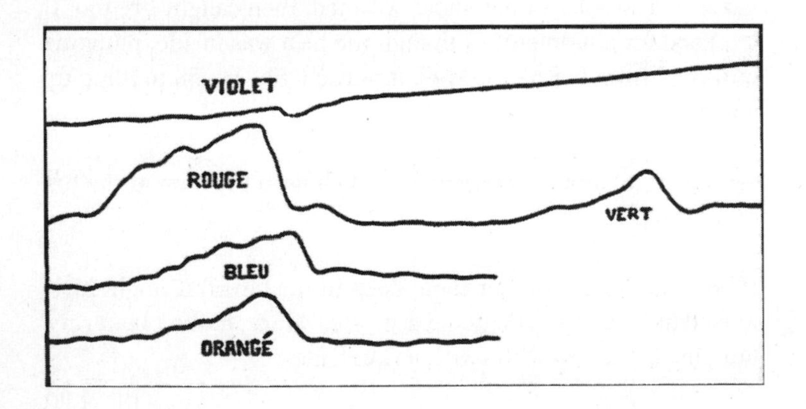

A Small Tree with Incredibly Long Roots

June is a doll with wide eyes. A child stands on tippy-toes. Wants her doll from the dollhouse on stilts.

The child loves to play with the June doll as if she were not a virtual pet but a live one... knocks her down and catches her. To the child – whispering into June's hair, watching the lashes close when she lays her down and, rushing back, finding her there, pretending that she never moved at all – to the child, June *is* real, as real as any real daughter. The child's fierce monkey love has breathed a kind of fabulous life into her.

The child gives June a kiss and croons, "Rock a bye bay-bee..."
"I'm not a baby any more," says June, brushing her teeth.
"You'll always be my baby," says the child, hugging her tight. "You'll always be my baby, no matter how old you get."
June runs her tongue over her teeth. They feel smooth.
"And down will come bay-bee, cradle and all!" sings the child.

June's lip is numb. The dentist taps her on the nose. "All ready," he says. June stares up at the cardboard ceiling, can see glue on the metal hinges where the roof lifts off, the paper-blue sky.

The child peers into the thirty-second-story window. "Don't hurt her!" she says.

With a surgical knife he makes an incision in the back of her mouth behind the molars. Eyes focused hard, he exposes the white of a wisdom tooth. "Bingo!" The dentist clamps the tooth. With enormous pressure it has started to force her front teeth to shift. It is growing in crooked. He groans, pulling with the forceps, putting all of his body weight into it.

"Awww," June moans. The dentist's face turns red. His arms begin to shake.

"Oh! My baby! Can't look!" exclaims the child, covering her eyes, peeking through fingers.

"Whew! It's a real fighter!" he says, stopping to wipe his brow. He puts one foot up on the chair for leverage.

"Awww!" June moans.

"Don't hurt her!" says the child, lifting the window higher and poking in a giant eye.

When June was barely new she broke a front tooth. The child cried tears to see the damaged beauty of her doll's perfect face. "It doesn't hurt," said June.

"It hurts me," the child bawled, blowing her nose. June watched quizzically, unable to understand why the child was sad.

It is all June can do not to think of her body's demise (the way the child loves her so hard): hair falling out in clumps from so much brushing, fragile teeth breaking, skin coloured with marker, lipstick circles around the eyes. But lying back with her mouth open, she has a small epiphany. Like all the other small Junes, she was not made to last forever (forever is a long time). It is a relief to suddenly realize that things are as they should be.

Outside, the child clings to the building and, in the distant sky, helicopters circle. June hears the tearing of flesh in her inner ear. A bead of sweat from the dentist lands on her bib, and bleeds a deep blue. It is the blue of ocean, the blue of spring. Triumphant, the dentist holds up the wisdom tooth. "Got her!" he pants.

The tooth is enormous. It is the largest tooth June has ever seen. It is a small tree with incredibly long roots.

"One for the tooth fairy!" cheers the child through the window. "When we go home we'll put it under baby's pillow!" June doubts that. With those thick, bone roots, it would never fit under a pillow.

"Oops, I missed a piece," says the dentist coming towards June again. She looks up in horror. "Pull your tooth, pull your leg," says the joker dentist, slapping his knee.

When June was pulled from the womb (they used forceps — clamped and yanked), she thought she felt the scrape of teeth against her face and down her back. She thought she could feel those terrible jaws that clench and catch, jaws that would not let go.

Rattle rattle, goes the tooth in the paper cup. *Rattle rattle.* June shakes it trying not to think about the hole, now beginning to throb.

"When you're happy and you know it," chants the child, elated now that the party will start.

God damn it! June thinks almost out loud.

"See you soon, June," chimes the receptionist, "Next appointment — six months." June rattles the tooth in the cup, tries a lopsided smile. *Rattle rattle,* goes the tooth.

The child lifts the roof off the building, reaches down, takes the tooth from June. "Come here, little one," she says, shooing away the fly sized helicopters. She kisses June on the forehead and waves goodbye to the dentist, already with another patient. "There, there, lovie," she says, stuffing June into a knapsack on her back, and skips away humming, the small, bloody, bone in her fist.

Under the Influence

Yes. She was. Afraid. Afraid that something *like* love would fall — a grand piano from the cartoon sky, or a funeral (her own) making her break all her promises.

Touch? The flesh, bruise-yellow, pinkish in places, and there, where you see the weight of nightmares under the eyes, spotted leopard or purplish velvet puffs. Belong to this? Brush up against it? Lashes flashing against skin as though the lightest kiss?

Yes, she was afraid. That something like this had been waiting for her. She would have to forget all she knew, begin again.

The hostess informed her guests: She didn't eat meat, nothing alive — no animals certainly. Nor would she eat plants, if she could help it. Chewing on leaves and sprouts, June fantasized about gorging on the leftovers, not of many (lovers) but one. Words always held a power if used with the breath rushing in, an inverse sigh, a boat flattening into... a spoon; ready to eat, yes, ready to lick the salt from each other's wounds, trashy vamps *(weren't they!)* and hungering for more.

That night they caught glimpses of each other in the crowd. They drank hard, and did not speak, left for separate rooms, or the garden where the air was cooler and bottomless.

Could not meet those eyes, wild as hanging gardens, wide as searchlights. Except when drunk. Yes. June was. Afraid that gaze might see right through her. Her own eyes, familiar as almonds, shot back in the bathroom mirror. June steadied herself. She thought she could see tiny hands in the folds of skin under her lower lashes. She had never noticed them there before. Were they made to catch tears? To clear away debris? She wanted to pluck them out with tweezers, examine them. They were miniature windshield wipers. She was thrilled, disturbed... too much to drink – when the door opened suddenly.

Both faltered, "Oh! I didn't know!" and the noise from the party rushed in, crushing, flattening into... awkward and mute, they stared at one another.

Just then, a phalanx of moths filled the open window, flitting beige, specked white and black, yellow, maroon... Saturnid. Ruby Tiger. Dark Arches. Silver Y. Moths brushing against arms, throats, thighs. Tickling. Heart and Dart. Yellow Underwing. Dingy Footman. Flame. They started to laugh, first giggling, then louder, until they bent over holding themselves, sliding down the wall onto the cold bathroom floor. Moths, kind of soft and eyelashy.

The Man with the Mustache

The sound of the truck gearing up in the alley edged her closer to facing things. The pipe exhaust had that long trip smell, overweight and greasy. He didn't know yet, would perhaps never know. She had betrayed him (the floor rippling under) with all the dullness of detail, and it felt bad being the only one who knew. When — if ever — she told him, he would feel stumps at the back of his eyes. But she wouldn't feel stumps at the back of her eyes. This is a thing to remember about pain.

When She is Dancing

When she is dancing she recalls nothing that has passed or that there will ever be a tomorrow. She is dancing, spliced, watching herself dancing, and dancing, swimming through crowds, and watching herself swim. She can groove, she can groove, yes, her skin is opalescent, wet with pearls of sweat, glistening under disco ball flicker as the band plays and the lady in red opens up her mouth for another ice-cream vowel, oooooooooooh. Arms swaying, hips rolling, eyes closed, she is invisible, indifferent, all vanities and insecurities have been doused like hydrants flooding a burning house till it drips empty, but now sure of its bones.

When she is dancing she is no longer a girl, a woman, a daughter, a lover, a liar, a sigh, a name. She is a corner of elbow, ankle, nose, she is a rubix cube, earlobe, thigh, she is belonging to nothing two-dimensional, as if belonging to a place before thought where sounds and colours merge and pulse and shift with the changing tune. She is a shade of rouge, of pinky yellow, of derelict taupe, all that swims and blends and swallows itself.

When she is dancing she dances alone.

When she is dancing she is closed, fenced-off land, she cannot be called back, as if dancing were trance, as if every note were moving forward beyond and the road falling away behind. For a moment she is that kind of chisel, and that kind of lost. Until she becomes something else. Buckled in under rhythm, drums and horns, and voice that sounds like electric violin and metal crushing, like the fluid in a leg, she is there draining. By the stage she is water and air — flutes — the way water and air can feel hot or thick, the way water and air can fill a cup or flow over. When she is dancing she is fine-tuned, like lips brushing lips or wings

just so

until the music... music?

There is no thing called music when she is dancing. The perfumed moon hangs in the distance, this is nothing to her — if there were gods she would not need them. When she is dancing she can smile and swim and need for nothing. She is yesterday's supper, in the way that it's forgotten. Small as the girl who is a whale. She slides down ladders and belongs to bridges.

When she is dancing she owns the kingdom. The sharks memorize their smiles in beforehand mirrors, but she has eyes the way glass eyes just look pretty, do not see. There in the sandy bar, in the velvet space coughing up horn and hammering strings, calling for some funked-up version of last era, she is not taken in, she is not taken for ransom, she is very fresh. (Are daisies fresh? Not as fresh. She has cheek. But give her shoes and she will topple.)

For all the times she berates herself, there never was anyone who could dance like this. When she is dancing she is at her deepest core, for all the hours that sit wanting — the flush on her — for the ugly and the bad and all that seems impossible, consumed, yes, she is a lovely hurricane. When she is dancing she loves the strength she has and loves the quiet hole inside, and she eats pigs and trucks and doors as if wind were a cello moving her.

she sells seashells she sells sea shells she
sells sea shells she sells sea shells she shells
she shells she sells sea shells she shells sea
shells she shells sea shells sea shells sea
shells she shells she shells she shells she
shells she shells sea shells she shells sea

shells sea shells she shells she sells she sells she sells she shells she shells she shells she shells she shells she shells she shells she shells

A Day at the Beach

Part 1.

She was very small. She dreamed a red liquid soaked her white, cable knit tights. She sat in the bath as the liquid turned the water into plumes of dark red. She didn't have the words for it, all she could say was that the dream made her feel "funny" inside. She had nightmares for weeks and didn't want to leave the house, even to play in the evenings with the children on the street. "They were bad, bad witches!" said her mother, kissing away tears, and June saw then a huge gulf between them.

June knew there were no such things as witches.

Her child heart forced on with torpedo will to inherit more secret knowledge. As if knowledge were something she could slip into rather than suffer.

The surf of danger seemed to touch only June. Playing in her room, the sunshine crept across the various surfaces illuminating the cracks in the ceiling, the spots where the wallpaper bubbled. Thc daylight moved across her toy shelves, landing at the end of each day on an old ventriloquist doll. The doll had a sinister grin that said: *Beware! Watch out!* She kept to herself, observing the distance between what things seemed and what things were. She saw that there was a terrible hatred inside her, inky and thrashing. She saw that there was a terrible weakness, leeching just under the surface.

Part 2.

One summer at the beach she made a friend. It was her first real friend. Sometimes it felt like the happiness from being with Bee would burst inside her.

That summer holiday the two of them did everything together, waking at dawn and dragging home at night, sunburned and covered in sand. They explored the tidal pools. Staring into these waters long enough, the invisible appeared in the shape of starfish, sea urchins, schools of transparent fish. So too, the inky feeling inside her had a palpable shape, she knew, only she could not yet see it, try as she might. At low tide the two girls turned over large rocks to find crabs scuttling into the murk of clay. Capturing the mean little beasts in their buckets, this was their favorite game: torturing them, poking their shells with sticks, letting them run free on the flat beach and grabbing them up again like gods, watching their mouths froth, their beady eyes poke. They could kill them if they wanted to. And did. June adored her friend all the way from her ponytail to her pink grand piano.

One day they fought. "That's my ginger ale," said June.

"Is not," said her friend, holding onto it.

"Is too," said June. They debated until Bee poured the soda into the sand. June stomped away, expecting her friend to run after her, begging forgiveness (which she would consider after deliberating for, oh, a few minutes at least), but when June turned around the beach was empty. The sandpipers waddled up and down with the water's swell, the tide erasing their footprints. The waves crashed on the sand. The ears in her ears heard it as though for the first time.

The following summer she ran up to the beach house expecting to find her old friend. A new family had come for the summer.

Part 3.

"Take off your clothes," he said. Things had become ugly very suddenly. Above the drone of the furnace she could hear the sound of the ice in his glass as he swirled it around. He said, "Nothing's changed. You're still the same person." He began peeling off his shirt. But everything had changed. She had cheated on him, though it was not that straightforward. He had betrayed her too. Even though there had been a mutual understanding, it had changed the taste of everything.

June took off her skirt. The man watched, lifting up his monocle and pursing his lips. Her stomach hurt. She was tired and cold and she didn't know what she was doing at his house. She tried to warm up to him, by talking, but she found she couldn't feel anything any more. He was speaking gruffly anyway — the liquor had blackened him, taken the gentleness and turned it to business. At the same time, he seemed almost frail. She slipped out of her underwear. Her body trembled under the bright, overhead light. There was a yellow stain on the ceiling, glowing.

She picked up her shirt again and started to slip her arms through the sleeves. "What are you doing?" he pleaded.

Part 4.

Sometimes when you completely open yourself to someone, their hurt passes into your body.

Part 3.

He was naked and, having rushed out without his monocle, almost completely blind. June ran with her coat still unbuttoned as he chased her down the block. The wind was hard at her back, a violent grip she could not shake off. He had stopped just behind a street lamp and was calling her name, the bleat of a fog-horn, a name that seemed to belong to someone else, not her own name, a name she could only connect with a deleted summer, a word that sounded like nothing that meant anything at all, gibberish, a ghost ship. *June... June....* She wanted him to go away, go away for ever, just let her be. Lungs about to break wide open, cold slamming into her in waves.

She slipped into an alley. *Goaway goaway.* A woman passed and stared at the man. For a moment it was almost as if they recognized each other. Then he bolted into the night.

June had forgotten to protect the friendship, put it first, always. But was this person a friend? She pulled her coat more tightly around her neck, and bent into the wind.

At the corner of her block she made a quick decision to take the alley. She would risk that dark corridor rather than take the long way around. She hurried past the side of the building, shuffling down the alley, looking at her feet. But something made her stop.

Two eyes had appeared in the dark path. It was the man with the monocle (without his monocle). He stood there. Waiting. His face twisted. A question on his lips.

A scream rose in her throat and pierced the air.

Part 1.

She lay beneath covers, her red chair propped under the door knob. She had unplugged the phone, double bolted the door, pulled all the blinds down as far as they would go. She lay rigid under the icy covers, her heart racing. She was afraid of the man. She was afraid of her best friend. Perhaps he was outside right then, lurking, trying to break in. Perhaps he was calling her, calling her up on the phone, putting it on redial and slamming it down when she did not pick up. Or maybe he was drinking, swilling back whisky, the daggers in his eyes growing as he plotted. She didn't care where he was or what he was doing, as long as he stayed far away. Shivering, she pulled the cold in tight around her body, tugging at the bedding. And then she breathed in, and smelled the red silk pajamas left behind a few nights before. They smelled of perfume and of dog and of cigarette. She had gone insane — yes, it was a beautiful way to begin.

If the Accident Will

"Exquisite pain" is the medical term for the location of a break.

— Sophie Calle

Just when she thought she had protected herself from everything her body betrayed her. She sat up in the darkness and felt an odd sensation. It was somewhere under the surface of skin, or no, it was vibrating through the skin itself, she couldn't be sure, but it was there: in her fingers, her chest, knees, mouth. It was her own body. It was suffering. It was suffering for her. In spite of her. She could feel it acutely, living — dying. There was nothing she could do to negotiate with it; it would not listen (though it had two ears). In the room and all around her, her body ached with this particular sensation. In the darkness she could not see anything. She could not see even her own two hands, but she could feel them there. She could *feel* them. The darkness was no longer an obstacle to knowing her body. Like a blind dog's tongue, this darkness granted her the most intimate intransigence.

She folded the sheet down, running her hand over its coolness. She then touched one finger to the other, feeling her nails, the shape of hand, the dip and rise of each digit, plying her palms together, squeezing one knuckle at a time to feel the hardness of bone there. She touched an eye, hesitated, touched the wetness of eye, touched bottom lip.

She must have been afraid. She continued reading: *hair bump nail dry hard dry hard*. She was anxious to know what it was she suffered from: *soft lash wet bump soft*. There was pain — that was certain. She moved her hand to the pain, holding it. She allowed the heat to transfer from her palms, caressing the pain. She could not stop touching herself. She moved her hands up and down. And although there were points when she could not bear it, she did not want it to end. It made her feel like screaming out loud — it was the most exquisite joy.

Glitter

He said, "Everything glitters but you." Later on he said he meant it in a nice way.

That day she had watched a film and the film began with a tornado and the tornado began with a boy stating that people had been split in half, and cows had flown through the sky, and bones were sticking out of people's legs, and necklaces could be found hanging on the branches of trees, and a lot of people had lost their fathers.

June sat on a couch and the man sat with his monocle across from her. Everywhere there were cacti, ferns, aloe, and even some garden herbs. It was someone else's place and he was taking care of it.

"Life is good," he said.

"Love is lousy," she answered, quoting a friend. They had been talking this way for some time.

Everything shone these days for the man. It was as though splinters of the sun were in his eyes. Everything (these slanted days) that moved or sighed, everything shone. "True holiness is in the ordinary," he said to her. She hated his proselytizing. But "up there" in his knowledge the man was unaware. While the world turned round and round, illuminated by the effervescent sun, one side was always dark.

There is a story about a publisher who produces pornography magazines in Braille, not only the text but the photographs themselves. Even more peculiar, if you were to flip through an issue, you wouldn't see a thing; the magazine is printed white on white. The pretty pink cunts, airbrushed skin, the silicone breasts with perky nipples can only be *sensed* on the page. It takes a deft hand to feel the curves and lines that sculpt the shape of each body, but as you come to know the girl on the page under you, finger her, run your hand over her sex and stroke her hair, carve out the shape of neck, the arch of back... eventually the paper will darken from your hand. Gradually, her image will appear.

"What kind of cracker are you eating?" June asked the man.
"The kind from the shelf," he said.

A truck with a loudspeaker passed in the street. All bells and whistles, a truck with slogans, that sometimes gave out coffee and books, bellowed out a garbled message.

"What was that?" he said.

"Something about saving yourself," she answered, vaguely. The truck's tin rumble clattered away just as the record finished.

"The music always knows when to stop," said the man.

It felt like a scene in a film. The man rubbed his eyes, cleared his throat. The needle dragged. June stood up and said she would go. The moment felt thin enough to punch a fist through.

An Exit Can Also be an Entrance Looking Back at the Light

She studies the arc of the donkey, memorizing it like a map of summer, or sky. Only it is winter, and she is indoors at a birthday party and the only thing she wants right now is pin the tail right there, right onto that strange, naked spot. She is certain she can do it. An older girl blindfolds her and twirls her around three times, sending her off with a ribbon in her tight fist. GO JUNE GO! Arm out, June marches forward, absolutely convinced she will win. But the space around her feels different with eyes shut, air thick as pudding. She gropes around where the wall should be. Loses her balance. No wall. Screams of glee. She takes another step. Bumps up against something, *There!* as everyone bursts into laughter — she hasn't pinned the ribbon to the paper donkey, she hasn't even pinned it to the poster. She has pinned it to the wall not far from the light switch. June doesn't win the prize. A fat girl wins. The wrapping paper is all done up with bows and stickers and pictures of dancing cows. June has a temper tantrum, leaving the party early, and is fiercely unhappy.

Drinking beer and eating from a jar of cookies — she is stuck like Winnie the Pooh in the rabbit hole after he eats too much honey. Sitting back, feet up on the kitchen table, she should be content, but she is not. In her kitchen, eating crumbs, she wonders where the entire world disappeared to and how she can crawl back out of this place she's gotten herself into. She figures that because of this state — a state of monotony, a half sleep — she will, in the end, live longer. Perhaps she will outlive everyone: her fifteen minutes.

Cloudy with a 30% Chance of Flowers

Host *(in a baritone voice)*: What an honour to have you with us today, June.

June (*modestly*): Well, thank you.

Host: What you've done is really... really something! .... it's hard to find the words!

June: Thank you, so much.

Host: This... small feat... has lead to so much. You must be pleased.

June: Oh, but I'm not alone in this, really – I've had my chair.

Host: And you've brought your chair with you.

June: Well, I'm sitting on her.

Host: Of course you are! And what a beautiful colour, that red. Reminds me of a raging fire.

June: Oh no – it's *Blood Red*. The can of paint actually reads *Blood Red*, if you can believe it. I polished her for your radio show. It was quite an effort, getting her ready. She has a mind of her own, you know.

Host: So I hear. There's quite a story behind this chair.

June: Oh, come on, I've seen nicer stools than this.

The chair tries to throw her. June kicks it with her heel.

Host: So now, where do you plan to go from here, June?

June: Well, I'll continue, I guess —

Host: Oh?

Chair: *Hic!*

The host raises an eyebrow.

Chair: *Hic!*

June: Yes, continue, as if pulled along by an invisible...

Chair: *Hic!*

June: Do you have a little water? Could I have that glass of water by your notes?

The host hands her the glass. June feeds the water to the chair.

June: Sorry, where was I?

Host *(checking his notes)*: You were about to say how interesting this all is...

June: It *is* very interesting! Isn't it? Here we are. Chatting. And about not much at all. And we only have — well, 15 minutes or so.

Host *(observing the clock):* Thirteen with commercial breaks.

Chair *(nearly tipping June over)*: Grrrr...

June *(bending down)*: Sweetie, it's not your turn now, it's my turn. The nice man wants to talk to me.

Host: That's alright, June. I'd love to hear what your friend has to say.

June: Oh, she has a very thick accent. She's French, you know. It's hard to understand her.

The chair snarls.

Host: I don't mind.

June *(shrugs)*: Fine then. But it's not always pretty, I'm warning you...

The chair remains quiet.

June: Go ahead then. It's your turn. Go on!

The chair remains quiet.

June: See what I mean? I'm not making this up, you know.

She leans down as if to listen.

June: Well, it seems, suddenly, she has decided to be shy. I do apologize. All she'll do is smile.

Host: Smile?

June: Smile for the microphone, love.

The chair beams. The host is caught off guard. The smile breaks him wide open. He is overcome.

June: Are you alright? You don't look so good.

The host tries to find his place in his notes.

Host: Can you – can you tell us more about the future, June, what it holds for you?

June: The future is for the birds!

Flustered, the host ricles through his notes. He runs his hands through his hair, trying to recover his composure.

Host: Ahem! Right! The birds. Ah-ha! Yes, I thought so. You're using old material.

June: I am?

Host (taps the page, proud): It's right here in, *June's Tea Party.*

The chair winks at the host and he pales. His hands skate across his knees

June: Really, what else does it say in those notes?

The host leans over. Ever so quickly, he brushes the side of the chair.

June: Can I see them for a minute?

The host lightly fondles the legs of the chair. June leans over and takes the notes from the table. She begins to read. A light above the door starts flashing on and off. The host's hand is covered in paint. Red paint spills over into pools on the carpet. Assistants rush in with towels, a mop. The host cannot take his eyes off the chair. He wipes one hand on his suit. An assistant runs over and tries to clean him up. He has paint in his hair, on his ears, across his neck. June reads, skimming the pages, biting her nails, mouthing the words. Mouthing the very words: biting her nails.

She Arrives in a Loose Burnt Skirt

It's a low-grade *buzz*, electricity charged by water, not brittle, dry wires. The oily, greasy, wool of hair and air. But it's not all burn and air, there's the limnetic earth, a grounding there. And a softness to her edges; turned inside-out, persimmon flesh. She reacts: to the bike with deer horns, *there was all this fluff covering his bike, his body, fuzz...* noting this at six. Now she is trying to catch the stuff when it passes through the light, stick it to tape, flypaper, sparks and ions, the soft *thwack* when a particle sticks.

She's spinning, plucking threads, hair, wool, fluff, dust, from the grass, from her head, the air, her coat; moves hand to mouth, tries to pull the shape of something out, fingers stop. Hover. Her hand falls (she's holding that thought down there by her belly, the place where vowels live).

She yanks hairs from her head, ties them together at the ends, pins the line to two opposing walls. The line is a map she drew in her sleep.

When the film starts it's a mouth sensuously kissing an arm, and then as it pulls back, body connects to head.

A lit match. Touched to the taut line of hair. *ping*. Walls fall down.

A Novel Feeling

This is the way it was for a while. Perhaps a lifetime if lifetimes are short and deliberate. When June felt her mother using her looks to live inside she beat it out of there. A home can be a box or a boxcar. Wished then to be moving, thumb out, ticket in hand; that was when she could think, hear her own mind hammering on — only with wheels underneath — then she knew she had a mind. It was a novel feeling.

It all started with the dream of something. She wanted to own a horse. Not a pony, but a real horse, a mare with a glistening mane she could comb and a coat she could brush. June wrote down a few words and posted the ad in the local newspaper. It read: *Will loan body for use of horse.* Imagine June riding her horse down the Main, bareback — not just trotting but full gallop, jumping cars, pedestrians, tables of fruit... It was a spectacular dream. *All you have to do is close your eyes.*

She's shy but won't show it; will sleep around to prove herself. They promised to lift her up, hold her high, but they dropped her instead and took everything away except the batteries. Dead batteries, that was all they left behind. In that squat there was a radio but it rarely had batteries. When it did though, it would play all night long.

In the alleyway, June has fallen in love again, with the dream of something.

She's lazy these days; doesn't want to read, doesn't want to work, no one ever taught her the dirt in her mouth won't grow gardens. Even though it's all staring her in the face like a bad Sunday afternoon soap opera. She is sleeping again because sleeping can be better than everything else. They don't advertise it because they don't need to.

She rode that horse all the way down the Main, and there was nothing then but black sky and a wonderful desperate feeling, like drowning.

The moon ticks past the tips of trees. The damp, dark scent of freedom. The steam of lather comes up hot like dope, the hiss of wind, cheek close to that sleek body, thighs, damp with sweat (hers... his), sound of hooves... She rides along the old highway road. Nothing can pin her down. Horse and rider move together as one, see as one, *sweat* as one. Because she has learned something that was, until moments ago, untenable. She feels emotion turning over inside her like the pages of a glossy magazine. The wind pushes her lips open, parting to dry teeth, skirt billowing up. She does not know what will happen next and she does not care. Everything has changed and everything is the same.

She would like to tell the old man
            that sex
      is not
                                    just another way of moving.

He is traveling too. Old, with his houses and cars and several ex-wives. He looks, right now, like a boy. He is in a rowboat and the oars crack his knuckles with each stroke. His lips look bruised, and the wind has blown away his hat, and it is as if his knees are too big — it's some kind of toy boat, shaped like a walnut shell. He just barely fits. He spins in circles, tossed by waves and his own indecision, stopping often to drink from a silver flask that he keeps in the pocket of his cape.

If June loved the man with the monocle, would it keep them together in some story-book way? Keep *her* together? That's what. Now that he's gone.

The boy at the bar tells June he likes abandoned buildings, the ones down by the river, near the market. He lives down there because he's poor, he says. He never tells June what it is he does to not make a living, but he does tell her that he would like to photograph those buildings as they are demolished, step by step — because wrecking is like building, he says. It's creative. Each demolition crew must choose to destroy a building in a certain and calculated way. It doesn't just all come crashing down at once. It's the way they take her down, beautiful blow by beautiful blow. Until there's nothing left standing. It's the most beautiful with very old buildings, or churches, he says.

Once Heard Opera that Sounded Like This

1. *flavus* = golden-yellow, related to white
2. *lividus*: Aristotle had this as equal to *flavus*, and a white, but it is also the colour of lead (which produced white lead), so it might be a dark grey as in 17 (later)
3. *albus* = white
4. *candidus* = shining white
5. *glaucus* (*karops* is Greek) = a yellow with more white than yellow and red in it; the colour of camel-hair
6. *ceruleus* = wax-yellow
7. *pallidus* = pale yellow
8. *citruinus*: doctors say that this yellow is reddish in urine. Avicenna says that it includes *igneus* (fire-colour) and croceus
9. *puniceus* = ?orange; [in Opus Maius VI, xii Bacon says that this is one of the grades of *glaucus* (5) of which the other is *caeruleum* (6)]
10. *rufus* = red-gold (?as in red-lead)

June's Birthday Gift

"Hey — look over there, that big yellow ball... it's a plastic ball with a small tumor ball inside!"

— Dan Gluesenkamp

For a long time there were birds. Birds of all kinds turning up at her feet, fragile but inert. Stiff bullets from the sky.

June woke from a dream, ill —
Puts a hand to the ache, a throb throb throbbing in her belly.

I am no longer June as I was this morning, she says, opening her front door. It is her birthday. She has become very old. She is so old she has no memory. She is perhaps one thousand years old.

Waking to find her body no longer her own.
Walks into sunlight
oblivious to cars
horns.

The doctor wanted to talk to her. *Uh oh,* thought June, wishing she could be carried away by a balloon, lifted off, holding onto the string. Sadly it is night again, the hardest time to be hard-boiled about anything.

"Where is your crown, mama?"

"Hush, now. I think I hear them coming." She holds a small child in her arms. He frees himself and wanders over to a book on the floor.

"Hop. Pop. Hop on Pop. Mama, give me a rhyme to rhyme with your name."

She gazes up out the window, "June. Balloon."

"June Balloon. June Balloon," and he laughs, "That's very silly." Then seriously, "Mama, my head aches."

"I know, lemon pie, there's nothing I can do."

"Rub it, please."

"Sweetheart, sit there like a good boy and read. Your head will stop hurting all on its own. It's a very clever head, you know." The boy smiles. "Here, give it to me and it won't hurt so much." The boy takes the crown off his head. It is a small crown made of brambles, string and glue, and bits of paper. It is a crown like any small child might make in art class. June places it on the sheet beside her. "But you must promise to be good and put it back on when they take you away."

"But... I don't want to leave."

"All children leave their mothers. You must be brave."

"But —"

"I don't want a fuss." The sound of a trumpet. "There now, shhh. They are coming." She hands him the crown. "Quickly! You don't want to make it worse." June wipes the blood from his forehead with the hem of her dress. "Now give me a big hug." He is glowing and so lovely. June has never felt a love this strong. She is trying very hard to be brave.

"Mama —" he wails as hands grab him roughly.

A mob has broken into the room, men and women shouting, arguing, uniformed members of the militia, trampling over *Hop on Pop*.

"Excuse us, Ma'am," says an officer.

"No!" screams the child.

"Let me escort you over here, Ma'am," says the officer taking her arm, "Best let them do their thing." He leads June over to a chair in the corner of the room. She watches, her face glazed white cherries. The little boy screams as they carry him out the door.

Her darling... Gone. Her lemon pie, gone. "You realize what you're doing," says June, looking up at the officer.

"We're just another army. Don't expect too much from us. We're just another army," he answers. She glances at the door. "It won't save him," says another officer plainly. "You know that."

A doctor is there in a leather skirt and white coat. "Scrunch down a little more, please. Good girl."

"I'm not... I mean – I'd hoped to ask some questions first," says June tentatively.

"Nurse." says the doctor. A young-looking nurse enters the room at a clip.

"He's an amazing child, really," June says as the doctor bends over her. "One in a million." The nurse wheels over a metal trolley. "You would like him," says June quietly, "He's special. Makes up stories, does tricks –"

"Okay, hon, you'll make this a lot easier if you just scrunch down some more, eh?"

"I can't hurt him," says June plaintively.

"Oh, this won't hurt," says the doctor, "It doesn't hurt this early on."

"No," says the nurse, "We caught it early. You won't feel a thing. One of the lucky ones."

"That's right," says the doctor, and with a wink she asks June to remove all her clothes.

June lies naked on the table. She would like a cover, but the nurse has vanished and the doctor has already begun. "A little wider, June." June opens her legs. The doctor touches her. "This will relax you," she says, and then her hand goes deep inside, thrusting, and she begins to kiss June's face. June squirms but the doctor continues to push her tongue into June's mouth until her body finally shudders in waves of pleasure, and there is the doctor smiling, "You have a beautiful baby boy!" The nurse hands her the child.

Blood beads in the tracks the brambles have left between June's thighs. Blood drips into the little boy's blinking eyes. June looks down feeling such a strong love it causes a second tremor inside. "Come back!" she yells to the staff who have left her alone with the infant. "Come back!" A bumblebee flies out of June's vagina. June begins to cry. Another bee flies out.

"Don't cry, mother," says the infant.

"But the bees," says June, tearfully.

"They are friends," he says.

June is bewildered, bumblebees flowing out of her like a mountain stream and buzzing in her ears, buzzing in a cloud above the bed, and June afraid of being stung, especially where she is so raw. "June, I presume," says the infant with a smile, holding out a hand. June is amazed. Just out of the womb, yet so articulate and polite. And, as if prompted, the infant begins telling stories, and performing tricks with a coin.

It is June's birthday and she is celebrating. "What a tiny thing you are," she says cooing, and reaches over to adjust his funny bramble hat. But boy and hat have disappeared down the long corridor, the swarm of bumblebees following.

"No hurry. Lie there until you feel more stable," says the doctor.

"You have someone taking you home?" says the nurse.

"Yes," June lies.

"You're sure," says the nurse.

"Yes," June lies.

"Okay then," says the doctor, "Get plenty of rest. Make a date for a check-up."

No, thinks June. "No!" she says aloud, now realizing what has happened, "Have you seen my little boy?" But the doctor is smirking. June stands up and feels dizzy.

Easy there

— says Nurse

helping her to her feet.

My clothes

— says June

Burned

— says Nurse

Don't want to contaminate you.

Of course

— says June
leaving the operating room with her sneakers in hand, trying to cover her breasts.

"Goodbye, everyone," June says to the lady at the reception desk, "They are sending me away."

"They send everyone away eventually, dear. Except for me. I never get to leave... someone taking you home?"

The automatic doors open for June, gleaming. "Oh yes," lies June. "My sweetheart."

Hot night of chills running through the blood. She is in a garden of snow under a half-onion sun. Thawing, in one dark patch, like a balding banker, the lake. And then she sees the others: a group of children frolic, laughing loud like men. They are swimming in the water where the ice has broken. June feels something in her arms. "Darling!" she says. Her lemon pie! He has returned.

Look at the small tumor she begot with the night. She rocks it in her arms. To June, it is the promise of a new beginning. This little thing — it is greater than anything else she has ever known (the hard edges that cut, ledge, floor, wall) — it is soft, squishy, it oozes with happiness, and... it is hers. Better than love, it is Grand Central Station; it is civilization's heir. Her heart wants to break. Hot hot and cold cold with each heavy breath. Sweat soaks the sheets. "Sweetheart," she groans, seized by cramps, but bites her lip. Good girl, June! Be a good girl, and soon he will come riding in and deliver you.

17. 

Note:
Complementary colours, when mixed in equal proportions, produce a grey that is vibrating and elusive, while a grey compounded of black and white is not.

Like Scarlett O'Hara

Quickly. Before she thinks. Nothing elaborate. Crust of bread with butter salt. But she thinks too soon and cannot eat. A red flashing light. Stop. Half done, pushes the plate away. Ravenous. It is a body closing doors, shutters, turning entire wings lead as if blood stopped there. Her body is law in the way it will not sleep, in the way it will not swallow. Cannot eat if she thinks and cannot stop thinking.

A cup. A stemware drinking glass. A tumbler. A mug. There is something that invigorates and intoxicates. Stops thought like bullets. Something made with ethers and esters. A variable colour averaging dark red. Wine from vines. Throat flushes open. A wine cellar is a room for storing wishes. The first dry taste is already too much. A sip of earthblood, mellow and heady trickling down, a hundred sensations traveling to corncob nerves. Colours like birds. A green flashing light beats like a heart in the costal cage. Later, other spirits; gin, tequila, whiskey. Colours strong as freight trains. Something that turns cold to honey. It's better to be dull and drunk and in the middle of a swarm. Stopped. When she drinks she doesn't think. Like Scarlett O'Hara she will think about it later. Like Scarlett O'Hara, there is nothing else written for her.

There was a mountain

There was a mountain. It had split. It was made of iron. A large round hill or mountain had split in two pieces, and there were arrangements she had to make to take care of it.

A tidal wave.
A dangerous cliff.

There was the great, tusked elephant swimming alone, deep underneath the surface of the sea with slow, ancient movements, and his wide toenails like lunar pies, paddling and middle grey, and serene.

This barren empty space. There were ashes strewn about.

A hurt animal lying on the road.
A gang of evil men.

There was the trapeze where she swung from above, taking point & shoot pictures. Below, the two in white taffeta ball gowns, in a ring like circus animals, about to be married off – both regal, their profuse skirts ballooning to the edges of the ring.

It was raining inside a sepia coloured house. Hot air balloons rose into the misty sky. She was moving inside, as if in slow motion.

The train enters the tunnel.
A huge tree has fallen down.

A drowning at sea.
Organ sounds come from far away.

There was a small girl singing with a wild, crazed voice. She joined in to sing *The Teddy Bears' Picnic,* meanwhile feeding the child a long, greasy sausage.

Her mother came and stood before her.
She was in a room of flowers.

There was a bus with the smell of perfume streaming out the windows and its wheels were melting.

In one of the flowers, tucked into the petals, there was a room of flowers.

Door
Number 1

that portion of the colour spectrum lying between green and violet
(when the sky turned)
[2]blue*n*1:

any of numerous small chiefly blue butterflies (family *Lycaenidae*)
(when the sky turned)
[2]blue8:

low in spirits: MELANCHOLY
(when the sky turned)
[1]blue3a:

Part Two

It was a Bright and (very) Hot Day

She gradually withdrew from that zone where things have a set form and edges, where everything has a solid and immutable name. Increasingly, she sank into that fluid region, quiescent and unfathomable, where clouds hovered, indistinct and fresh like those of dawn.

— Clarice Lispector
Near to the Wild Heart

(

A confession.

She loves you.

There. She has told you. Finally. It frightened her to say this much. She is not always so forward. Certainly, she is not always this whorish with her love. But it's true. And this time it's different.... The details don't matter; she loves you, regardless. She trusts you. Needs you. Enjoys watching you. Most of all, she believes in you.

Love is an act of faith.

What follows is intimate. It has not yet happened, though it has already passed out of memory, the way tears spill but do not stain. At the same time: this is not a self-help chapter.

What follows was written between the pages of sleep. Saliva blots the pillowcases — wet rings where seepage occurred.

Now, close your eyes: you will see the flicker of light passing through ribbons of celluloid. You will see the most luminous sky hung with one colour: blue. You will see wreaths of cloud and even the odd bird flying. And, looking in this heat for a water fountain that actually works, you will come to know the meaning of thirst.

It was a bright and (very) hot day. April, May... June. An end and a beginning.

Now. Close your eyes. Whatever it is you think you hear, stop your ears. Travel below. Understand that trains are deaf.

What you sense: that she has left her mouth on you.

Note: this chapter is but a parenthesis

THE WAY A STORY WOULD GO

Squinting, the sun had already burned through her chest, leaving a tiny hole. It was much too bright and (very) hot. The humidity knew to drag her to where only the ocean measured time. First foot on the beach and she wanted to run, leap, dive into the shimmering crinoline skirts of that Victorian mother. But as much as she wished to escape, she also wanted to be *there* under the sun — out, exploring, meeting people, tasting new and exotic foods. After all, this was her holiday. She was away from the encroaching walls of her winter apartment, having left ice for sand. It was as though a mystery — she hesitated to think — impenetrable and sooty, has smudged itself on the breeze. As if something, having taken her so far away to this strange new place, was about to happen. But she didn't believe in fate. She didn't believe in revelations or visions, even here. And yet, why *here*?

Sand ran through her toes. A film crew was setting up on the beach for a shoot. Their lights and stands and gear were all sectioned off with flags. A black actor in a cowboy hat stood smoking."

It was the middle of the day, high noon, but June had the intense sense of loneliness that usually comes with darkness. It was as though she had landed on the other side of the world where everything was the opposite from what she knew (day — night, happiness — grief, freedom — claustrophobia). At the same time, this feeling gave her a sense of herself: it gave her a bold security. And that ashen hole that had been burned through was helping her breathe more deeply.

The customs officer had asked the purpose of her trip. *Business or pleasure*. "Pleasure," she answered, perhaps too quickly. But he had believed her. But pleasure does not last. Perhaps she would find something indelible down there before returning home.

That is the way a story would go.

HOW TO WRITE A HOLLYWOOD SCREENPLAY:

1. The most important scene is the first scene. Grab the audience *by the balls*.

2. Keep syllables down to a minimum.
3. Keep everything generic. It's not a *brick* wall, it's just *a wall*.
4. Don't be poetic! Americans are violently opposed to poetry.

True story?

THE PROBLEM WITH TRUE STORIES

He said, "The problem with true stories is they always end in death."

THE WHITE BUS

Bus back to the hotel collides with a car on the wrong side of the road. The boy, a tourist, had been drinking. He didn't even think... (left side/right side, another opposite to contend with). Lip of boy split to gum. Face covered in blood as the colour drains to pale. They'll have to do some neat plastic surgery to fix all that. *If he lives*. Legs crushed by the engine's weight. *Legs jelly*. He thought he was just driving back to his hotel. They said he was there for a convention or something. He was working for some company.

5. Don't kill off the protagonist unless you have *a damn good reason*.

Passengers lying on the pavement like blown newspapers. Some wandering disoriented. Driver moaning with broken arm. Bone pokes under the skin of his wrist. One woman feels fine, won't sit down. Seconds later, faints. Hurled against the window of the bus, June lies prone on the side of the road.

the white of page
matches her face
face glowing moon

Ambulance wailing, ghost songs.

At home it might not have seemed so melodramatic.

Had she asked for too much?

Had she asked for some little story to happen?

ROUND

A motorcycle skids to a stop. Saw pain moving beneath the trees. Could be where the actor first found June — eyes closed asleep. A magician, decided to play god. Had taken first aid in school. Resurrect? It could be here that June first began to resist becoming human. Wanted to die (an angel) then.

Was stopped.

A sink of water. Held to evaporate slowly over time, not drain all at once. Might actually have been the magician lying there on the pavement, face black as the black of ink. (Face black as the back of moon.)

Magicians move mountains, produce flowers out of thin air, can take a drowned cat: give it life.

It was ridiculous when it happened finally, staring death in the face. It was ludicrous, that one could feel its shiftshape with all the trappings of life still within reach: a Walkman, a floral dress picked out with Hillary, the roughness of the road against her cheek. To be dead. What was that?

There were ants on her legs. Thought she might have things to do. Brush off the ants, for one. Or love. (Love, the poet has said, is a woman's whole existence.) But love would take her somewhere else. Writing love songs perhaps. As if hymns could take the ache of life and death away. As if life would be better this time round. Round and filled out. Like a page of moon. Rewritten. Not that there had ever been a beginning.

And so she named it: Round. Like a jar opening.

An imperative: the story must sound like it is going *there. In that direction.* So that when things become unbelievable or the story falters, one will keep believing.

Love is an act of faith. He said this at the end of a long relationship. He said, *You can tell a lot about a relationship by the way people say goodbye.*

At the end... how to say goodbye?

A little dying to make us all more palpable. Or immortal. Though did she hear you do not believe in heaven and hell?

June hoped the sensation of drowning would soon turn off like a switch and she would be able to sit up and stretch. Water threaded through her, murmuring its lullaby. She found a shape there. Just the shape of a girl.

The woman asked, "What kind of story will it be? She goes down to an island in the tropics, and when she arrives she sees that they are making a feature film there?"

"Something like that," she said.

FADE IN:
EXT. BEACH TERRACE — DAY

LADY

Yes but, I'm afraid to go. I had an aunt who went once. But I believe I'd be in danger. I'm having a bit of performance anxiety.

MAN

What do you mean?

LADY

How does that saying go? *No one really knows anything*. No, it's, *No one really does anything*. Know what I mean? It chooses for us. IT chooses for us. I want to live my life but it chooses my life.

MAN

You sound like Kerouac —

LADY

What else can you tell me about what you've read?

MAN

Oh, I'm interested in how people just know things, a shoemaker or boxmaker. We all know something, have our interests. I know how to build a miniature ship model, I mean that's something I know, how to make a cup of coffee, wash dishes, there's that kind of knowing how to do things... I mean, what's my question? I see myself trying to figure out what to say.

LADY

Most people think you have to say something.

MAN

It's getting late. We should go.

LADY

I'll go when I'm ready to.

Says, "I'll go when I'm ready to."

This. This is when June walks into the action, passes in front of the camera lens (picks up a shell, lets it fall). A cloud frames her from behind — or is that the smoke from a cigarette? This is what she looks like. This. Is what she looks like.

6. The production company owns the rights to your script throughout the world and THE UNIVERSE. It says this in the contract.

Night jasmine strutted its stuff and a scent even more impetuous: gardenia, white as smut. Here, where the humidity left a stain on anything, only the tropical flora was spared. It might as well have been a whole other universe — for all she knew about the world. And the mythic landscape that is geography.

Thumb out.

She would like to be running from something. If she were running from something specific she would feel like a heroine in a film. Lawless. Unskirtable. Able to shake down fences with her two bare hands.

June was beginning to recall a narrative. Somehow these thoughts were related to a trajectory. Not a clear trajectory, but the glimmers of one. Something familiar, something to call her own. But these relationships between things, this was not a narrative. No, there was something else. Something that told her...

but it glimmered far off, that answer of a thing.

Tried to move. Thought she knew how.

That was when he appeared without a sound. Startled her with a flower. Drowning white. White on white on white.

Bone wings.

Drum skin.

Petal.

Home was nowhere then.

EXT. OCEAN – DAY.

The cowboy walks out of the ocean carrying a conch shell. A young woman is sunbathing. He offers it to her.

COWBOY

In terms of rating saints and their miracles, after *Coming Back To Life*, *Breathing Underwater* would rate pretty high.

And then a black thing crawled out. Glistening.

Glistening!

(Nanny had let the cockroach out. Out of its matchbox bed.)

Black pearl.

It glittered past moon.
It had wings!
June believed in it then.

Because she wanted to believe. It did not mean believing would be easy.

(handwritten, the page slanted up to the right. hopeful.)

7. Three spaces between scenes. Readers love white space.

And, with believing, her body resurfaced. It took a moment to absorb the shift. The green ink of water to the new light of day

(

)

looked almost real then,

as if the brilliant rays were sunshine, not gels and flags and floods.

DOOR NUMBER 1

The blush rising to her cheeks
        could feel the heat on the road, under.
        could feel the hearts of sleeping mongrel dogs, miles off.

June was thirsty. The way the desert makes you thirsty. Here was a desert flooded with water she could not drink.

There was a secret now, a mystery (life), something almost tangible. She was beginning to sense — what? Failure. No, not failure. Falling. No, not falling, exactly... the feeling of being herself... whatever it was, it felt legitimate, her birthright — *she* felt legitimate, could assign a spool to the thing inside — was this all there was then?

Shhhh, the sound in her ear.
Shhhh, the sound in her ear's memory. (Was the sound the dark ocean made when it breathed.)

...should have known not to ask what
                was behind door number 1.

The door swung open. Two eyes blinking.

And then —
The whiff of something familiar, curling in her nostrils, something that smelled like...

    (she swam through)

A man was watching her. And he was smoking.

At first, he appeared as a cardboard cut-out, edges glowing incendiary. A god on fire. Featureless, he reached out to take her hand. To take her hand. A gesture that simple.

Then he shifted. And the once eclipsed headlight blared.

And he was just a man.

"Looks to me you could use a nice, cold glass of lemonade."

A (mad)man. Thought he was a cowboy. Some magician! His whip cracking the air as he revved the bike, leaning hard into turns, speeding past stretches of vagabond beach. The night lunging past, wind in her eyes, June was a rider by an ocean that was once a desert, on a road that was once a jungle, on a bike that had the scent of life born into its metal flanks. A magician, a cowboy, an actor, the shiftshape itself! She was born with a love and that love had taken her here.

8. All stories are about a knight, a princess and a dragon. See *Peewee's Big Adventure*.

She was beginning to recall some small story. Some beginning perhaps? But the perceived shape of things did not fit with the things themselves. Square blocks in holes. The facts poured out, melting like waves before her. She could not remember what it was she was doing in this place.

The mid afternoon air was pungent with the smell of mangoes, papayas, ripe and rotting, over which swarmed billions of ants. Somnambulant, drilled by the heat, June walked a jagged line to the sea. The slurry tide. Left the strained air for the water's couch. Was this life again, then? Something so artfully simple.

The waves lapped a froth.

transported

All this. As if to say:

run — jump — fly

Her bobbing shadow sticks

June had not lost her memory, she had discovered a poetics. She had moved away from a script into fathoms of wine dark sea.

Waves sucked at the black shoreline. Calypso played on the ter race where painted ladies and men in floral shirts guzzled daiquiris and umbrella drinks. The truth was, no matter what had been stated, no matter what had been written, she despised him. Derided him. He was pathetic. He was stupid. He made annoying observations. He was everything she hoped never to be.

"Come here," she said. And kissed him.

That is the way a story would go.

9. No cursing. Three *fucks*, you cut off half the audience.

A DROWNING GIRL

When June grew up she would not swear. She would not wear high heels. She would not dye her hair. When she grew up she would be a kite. The sky was bigger than the sea. Kite ruffling in the dip of wind. She liked to climb trees. Enough sky for it. Like a man. Like the man inside her.

)

Coda

In the future

In the future humans will be able to arrange a beautiful sky. A beautiful sky should continue, an intense sky, a sky spun out, the slow float upwards of it, five thousand billion acres of shades of azure and aquamarine, each piece of sky a perfect bruise blue.

In addition to the constant sky, the birds tumble through, cutting rivulets of air with a slice, a slash. Suddenly, a red-tailed hawk tumbles, falls. Then, the explosion of blood vessels, like marks under skin, as happens to bodies. Isn't a bird-torn sky a better sky? The blue black mark, the red mark, is there in the sky like a hard kiss. Carries the sky in again. There is no second sky. Only one constantly bruised blue.

There is therefore no reason to vote for anything else. The difference between the moon, the sun — do not vote against the sky. The beautiful sky should continue. It will not survive harsh criticism. It is equally distributed throughout the world. It either will or will not be a beautiful sky. The population might reason the sky unbeautiful. But the latitudes covering meadows for only six weeks would know their decisions about blossoms, and would vote "sky." In Antigua, Ireland, Siberia, would vote "sky."

It would not be surprising if the ground beneath the sky glows because the constant sky has no self interest. Because the same constant sky, like a kelp forest, has been informed of a loss.

Black, wide, pulsing winter nights, summer days. That sunrise and sunset perceived themselves as part of a life support system.

The clouds, shredded from wing, were wind pasted back together — bears, sheep, cuddly creatures. The same seems likely to occur again.

AMANDA MARCHAND is a Montreal writer and photographer based in New York. She has recently completed a two-year residency at the Headlands Center for the Arts, and holds an MFA from The San Francisco Art Institute. This is her first book.